Jocelyn LaFavers

A Christmas Killer

To all the Christmases that have ever been and ever will be.
May God bless them—every one.

"I will honour Christmas in my heart, and try to keep it all the year. I will live in the Past, the Present, and the Future. The Spirits of all Three shall strive within me. I will not shut out the lessons that they teach."

EBENEEZER SCROOGE, A CHRISTMAS CAROL —CHARLES DICKENS

Contents

PREFACE

This book is inspired by the incredible Charles Dickens and his wonderful novel, "A Christmas Carol", the reading of which has long been one of my favorite Christmas traditions. While I could never begin to live up to the standards set by such an incredible author, it is my sincerest pleasure to be inspired by him, and by the characters he created, turning a ghost story into a mystery that hopefully continues to entertain others and inspire the Spirit of Christmas itself. I challenge you, dear reader, to look for my nods to Dickens at every turn. I also advise you to take the title of this book seriously and read with caution. If you are unsure that you can handle mild descriptions of violence and blood, then this book is likely not for you. Please also be aware that to keep with the original story that Mr Dickens so artfully crafted, there is mention of death, child loss, and grief. As you lose yourself in this cozy mystery, I hope you also find yourself.

 Acknowledgments

A long, long time ago, God gave me a passion for writing, which has never faded. It is my sincerest hope to give Him glory in everything that I write. I could never have accomplished this work without the many people who have encouraged me along the way; particularly my husband, who never, ever, ever let me give up and tells me every day that I am a great writer, my kids for putting up with all of my distracted, harebrained story chatter, Amanda Godin, who always believed in me, and Greg Wood, whose idea inspired this story in the first place.

Stave 1: Marlene's Ghost

Marlene was dead: to begin with. There was no doubt whatever about that. Eve had watched in numbed horror as the paramedics took away the body. Had stood in the freezing drizzle with Marlene's parents and brothers whilst the undertakers lowered the casket into the ground. Had packed up her friend's belongings into cardboard boxes so her parents would not have to see what Eve had seen inside their dorm room. Marlene was gone.

Eve sat alone in her dreary London office, completely ignoring the lovely soft snow that fluttered down, coating the entire world outside in a layer of white, the dirt of the city now hidden from view. Her computer screen was aglow with rows and rows of numbers, a cold representation of consumerism's control over the modern world and, by extension, over Eve herself. Another smaller screen lit up the room, the name of her assistant appearing on the glass. She sighed impatiently and swiped the screen with her finger to answer the call, bringing the device up to her ear.

"Yes, Babs?"

A strange, wet honking sound blasted over the airwaves, causing Eve to distance her smartphone from her ear for a moment, disgusted by the revolting noise.

"Sorry, Eve," the owner of the voice on the other end of the line sounded miserable and tired. Her throat was full and gravelly, and her words sounded as if they were coming through her nose rather than her mouth. "I've got someone on the other line for you who says they know you from school."

Fantastic. She narrowed her eyes suspiciously. A school "chum" trying to reconnect, probably going to ask for some kind of discount on her accounting services. None of them had really liked her back in school, so why would they pretend to feel differently now that they were all grown up? No one had ever really given her the time of day. No one except Marlene.

"Patch them through, Babs," she sighed impatiently. A yucky sniff preceded a distant click that sounded as the line switched over, and Eve put on her smoothest, most professional tone. A stark contrast to the ailing voice of her faithful assistant. "This is Evelyn Scrooby."

"My word, Eve, you sound so grown up! The years certainly have flown by, haven't they?"

The overly cheery voice grated on Eve's nerves, already raw from a long day staring at a computer screen. She closed her eyes, rubbing the lids with her fingertips.

"I'm sorry, I'm afraid I don't recognize your voice straight off. Who is calling, please?"

"Oh, Eve!" The voice grew teasing and more sickening with false sweetness. "It's Janine from secondary school!"

Oh, yes. Janine Richards. Janine, who led the pack of popular girls, flipping their blonde locks in superiority as they passed their social victims in the corridors. Janine, who dated the most athletic boy in school and made sure that everyone knew that he belonged to her. Janine, who never seemed to have a single flaw about her and got everything she could ever want in life without putting in an ounce of work for it. That Janine.

"Hello, Janine, it's been a long time."

"It has, indeed! I hear that you are a big-shot accountant now with your own firm and everything. It's so wonderful that you've accomplished so much!"

In spite of everything, Janine was implying. Eve could read between the lines.

"Yes, hard work certainly gets you places. How can I help you, Janine?"

"Well, my husband and I have adopted a charity for Christmas—you remember James—"

Oh yes, so the two lovebirds had created a permanent nest together, had they?

"Anyway, we are collecting donations for families affected by violence, and—well, I thought you might like to make a donation in Marlene's name."

Eve's stomach lurched at the mention of Marlene, unprocessed grief churning inside of her like a barely contained magma that longs to break through the surface of the earth. Marlene had been the one friend who stood by her when her parents died, and she got passed from foster home to foster home until they were old enough to go out on their own and go to university together. The only friend that ever seemed to care about her had been snuffed from her life, like a glass lamp violently thrown against the pavement.

"What on earth would a donation from me do for someone?"

"Well," Janine's sickly sweet voice faltered, as if she did not expect such a biting response. "The donations do lots of things. They might pay an electric or gas bill. They might buy groceries or a few warm coats for winter. We just try to show people that someone out there still cares for them, you know?"

"Aren't there still foster homes? Doesn't the government already grant assistance funded by the nation's taxpayers? If so, let them beg their help somewhere else."

"There are those things, yes, but—many would rather die than take those routes."

"If they would rather die, then they should hurry up and do it, and decrease the surplus population. You don't need my help to prolong their debilitating misery."

"Do you prefer that we keep your donation anonymous?" Janine continued to push Eve's buttons.

"I wish you would leave me alone," her response escaped her clenched teeth like a vicious growl. "Good day."

"Eve, I didn't mean to—"

"Good day, Janine."

With that, Eve's finger angrily jabbed at the red circle on her screen. It took her a few stabs at the glass to end the call successfully, stoking the flames of irritation even higher before the line was finally closed. She grunted with bitter satisfaction and slammed the device down onto the desk in front of her. Today, as always, had been a terrible reminder of the Christmas Eve seven years ago when she had walked home from work, singing carols all the way, only to step into her university dormitory room and find her best friend brutally murdered. There had been blood everywhere, but Eve had knelt on the sticky floor to scoop up her friend's limp body, desperately searching for any sign of life. Her screams had alerted other students, and someone had called 999. She was still attempting artificial resuscitation when the paramedics arrived, although it was far, far too late for the beautiful young woman who lay motionless on the floor. The room was otherwise filled with signs of Christmas cheer, wrapped packages stacked neatly on a bed, a small artificial Christmas tree covered in tinsel, and twinkle lights adorning a desk in front of the window. It was a macabre scene that Eve felt she would never be able to erase from her mind, and even now, she could nearly feel the terrible warmth of Marlene's blood on her hands, her lifeless body heavy and pale in Eve's arms.

Eve released a shuddering breath that she had not realized she'd been holding in and angrily swept tears from her cheeks with the cuff of her shirtsleeve. Attempting to calm herself down, she reached out a shaky hand to the pile of mail stacked on a corner of her desk. It had been accumulating there for at least a week, and she had been avoiding it like her ancestors had probably once avoided the plagues of London. A cheery red envelope with familiar handwriting caught her eye, pressing pause on her disinterested flipping through the pile and setting the others down, forgetting them altogether. Opening it almost reverently, she drew out a lovely card decorated with a Christmas scene one might expect to see on a television ad meant to inspire feelings of nostalgia: a horse-drawn sleigh pulling a jovial couple through the snow. Inside the card was a kind note requesting that she join the writer for the holiday's festivities. The same sort of correspondence came every year, and for the last seven years, Eve had refused the invitation. At first, she had sent back RSVPs declining the invitations, but soon enough, she simply stopped responding altogether. It had become too painful to even consider gathering in a room with happy party-goers when she wasn't at all happy herself. Eve didn't even think that most of the people in attendance would want her there to spoil their merry-making, anyway. All the same, the sender continued to invite her every year without fail. Eve's throat thickened, her eyes pricking annoyingly, and she tossed the card into the rubbish bin on the floor beside her desk. She stared gloomily at the card for a moment before reaching to pluck it out of the bin. She pulled open the bottom drawer of her desk and shoved it into the growing pile of greeting cards at the back of the space—all seven years' worth of them. Staring at the stack of brightly colored correspondence, Eve could feel her sense of gloom growing stronger by the second, and she pushed the drawer closed with a not-so-gentle shove, a satisfying *whack* resounding in the room. Enough of working today. She was going to bed. She picked up the loathsome smartphone and dialed her assistant's number back, a call which was answered after a single ring on the line.

A rather croupy cough punctuated the answer at the other end of the line."Yes, Eve?"

"It's Christmas Eve, Babs. Might as well call it a night."

"Thank you, Eve. Will you..." the voice grew hesitant at the other end of the line. "Will you be needing me tomorrow?"

"I suppose not," Eve groaned out her response, conveying the inconvenience she felt at Babs' hopeful inquiry. "You're going to want to take off for Christmas Day, aren't you?"

"Only if it's convenient, Eve! I—I can always put my phone on silent and answer anything via text message if that is alright with you."

"No, I suppose you might as well take the day since you work from home, anyway. I'll slave away here by myself. Just report all the earlier the next morning, if you can even get out of bed after all your merriment."

"Of course, Eve! I'll call you first thing on the 26th! Thank you so much! Merry Christmas!"

Before Eve could respond with a snarl, her assistant had ended the call, a very wet sneeze interrupted by the beep of the disconnecting line.

Bah.

Eve shut the laptop on her desk with a snap, the eerie glow suddenly ceasing to illuminate the darkening room. She walked to the window, peering out onto the street below, where snow continued its gentle fall in the growing moonlight.

Humbug.

Her stomach rumbled, demanding her attention. Taking her phone from the desktop, she pulled up the app she used to order food and tapped the "reorder" button. She didn't like change very much, and consistency suited her. She absentmindedly scrolled through the news articles on her phone for a few moments before casting the device aside in annoyance altogether, choosing to wait for her food in the silence of her office. Her order did indeed arrive quickly, as Simpson's Tavern was just at the corner of her street. Soon her digital doorbell chimed, prompting a notification to pop up on her phone's screen. When she opened the app, a delivery boy stood annoyingly close to the camera, whistling *"God Rest Ye Merry Gentlemen"* directly into the microphone.

"Put it down and go away!"

The poor youth, who must have been around sixteen, jumped in fright, nearly dropping the paper bag containing her meal from his hands. He quickly deposited the bag on the stoop before dashing away in the snow, more frightened than a cat with a barking dog at its heels.

Eve trudged downstairs and opened the door to find her soup tipped over and leaking into the paper bag. Slush and ice began soaking the bag from the outside in.

Bah.

Stupid teenager.

As she stepped beyond the threshold and bent over to pick up her quickly cooling supper, the heavy wooden door blew shut behind her, bumping into her and nearly knocking her into the snow.

Humbug.

Turning around, Eve jumped back a few steps, astonished to find that the antique door knocker, which ordinarily looked like a lion holding a curved bar for knocking in its iron jaws, now took a different form, as if by evil design. Her heart seemed to halt its duties, taking on a stony weight in her chest, but she couldn't tear her eyes from the changed door knocker in front of her. The object had assumed the face of her old friend, dead these seven years. A blank stare emanated from the face, its skin glowing with a green, ghostly pallor, as strands of hair floated about it, framing the terrifying visage. Eve stood frozen, staring at the old knocker now transformed until momentarily it opened its mouth in a terrifying whisper, speaking Eve's name mere inches from her face. The whispered words swept across her features like an icy wind, and Eve jumped back in horror, nearly dropping her soup in fear. She rubbed her eyes with her fingertips, and upon opening them again, found that the door knocker had once again taken its original form. No light emanated, no face from the past, no floating hair surrounded its form. With a trembling hand, Eve turned the knob, but not before inspecting it thoroughly to ensure that there was nothing amiss with it.

Still cautious, she stamped her feet against the door frame to remove as much of the dirty London snow as she could before stepping inside the antechamber of her home, finding it now darker than before. Sure that she had left the light on before retrieving her supper, she pressed the button on the wall into the *on*, then *off* positions several times before giving up altogether. Blast these old London row houses! Even the once-grand ones were such a drain on a person's bank account. She would have to have an electrician out yet again, but she would wait until at least the day or so after Christmas, or she would end up paying an exorbitant premium. She could stand having a dark entryway for a few days to keep from being charged a cost equivalent to her right kidney in holiday surcharges. She pulled her smartphone from the back pocket of her jeans and turned on the flashlight feature, casting its beam on the wide staircase before her. The old house was as dark as a tomb with no lights, and the staircase was so broad that she would have nothing to grasp at if she took a tumble down the stairs. Once in her bedroom, she attempted to turn on the lights in there, only to discover the same problem as in the grand entryway. Rolling her eyes and groaning in aggravation, Eve heaved a massive antique wing chair closer to the gas fireplace and turned up the dial to make the flames just a bit higher. She propped her phone up against a dusty vase containing a long-withered bouquet in an attempt to further illuminate her supper. Pulling the plastic container from the bag bearing the logo of the public house she always ordered from, which was now entirely falling apart, she saw that between the boy's clumsy placement of the parcel on her stoop, and her own clutching in fear at the sight of her door-knocker, nearly half of the small portion of soup had spilled into the bag, leaving her with a meager

serving of now-tepid chowder. The bread that
had accompanied her meal had thankfully soaked
up most of the liquid, so there was at least that.
Digging around for the plastic spoon and napkins
that should have been in her order, Eve found that
she was left wanting. The blasted delivery boy had
either dropped them along the way or some dolt
at Simpson's had forgotten to put them in the bag
altogether. She leaned against the chair's plush back
for a moment, trying to decide if she wanted to
make the trek downstairs to the kitchen for a spoon
when the bluish beam coming from the back of the
device she'd positioned on the side table suddenly
gave up the ghost. Frantically, Eve checked the
screen, only to find that the flashlight feature must
have drained the battery entirely, and now that the
electrical was on the fritz in her home, she had no
way of recharging her phone.

Bah. Humbug!

She tossed the phone back down on the side table
next to the vase, leaving a small trail of distur-
bance in the layer of dust that had accumulated
on the wooden surface before greedily slurping
the remainder of the now-cool soup from the little
Styrofoam dish, pushing the soggy bread into her
mouth after it. An un-ladylike belch forced its way
up; a result of the hurried consumption of her meal.
Eve glared into the fireplace for a few moments,

mentally calculating how much more her gas bill would probably amount to since she would need to turn it up to use as both heat and light. The lack of electricity would likely balance it out on another bill, but then she would have the outrageous charges from the electrician to pay for. A sneer twisted her lips at the thought of the balances she would calculate on her personal accounts by the 31st of December.

A ringing in her ears began to distract Eve from her mental mathematics. Sticking a finger in the offended orifice, she wiggled it around in an attempt to break up the infernal din, but found that it was only growing louder. Looking around the room, her eyes landed on the set of butler's bells on the wall by the door. They started off swinging slowly, then increased in both their rate of swing and in volume until the noise was utterly deafening. Eve clamped her hands over her ears in an attempt to drown out the intonation, but just as suddenly as the ringing began, it also ended. The dust that was previously shaken off of the bells now danced around the room, illuminated by the flames in the fireplace and casting a ghostly pallor in the atmosphere. Nervously, Eve turned toward the bed, retrieving her pajamas from their place under her pillow, then spread them on the fireplace grate to warm before putting them on. While she waited, she paced anxiously. Her eyes scanned the room with suspicion until they landed on a photo in a place of honor on the mantle. Behind the dust-coated glass, two fresh-faced girls smiled at the camera, one of their arms outstretched to hold the smartphone the picture had been taken on. A miniature Christmas tree festooned with ribbons, baubles, twinkle lights, and homemade ornaments was beside them, standing in a place of honor on the desk by the only window in the tiny space. A photo taken on December 23rd, seven years ago. The day before everything changed for the worst.

"I can't believe you've been gone seven years today, Marlie," she reached wistfully toward the smiling faces frozen in time. "Seven years without answers."

"Seven years without justice."

Eve jumped so abruptly that she nearly left her skin behind, turning toward the new voice in the room with a jerk. Blinking hard, she stared at an apparition standing, nay, *floating* among the dust motes, mere feet from where she stood now clutching the ornate mantle for support. Reaching behind her, Eve groped for the fireplace poker on the hearth.

"Who are you?"

The figure before her was pale, a greenish light glowing from its shape, much like the one on the door knocker only a little while before had. With all the strength she could muster, Eve pulled the sharp implement from behind her back and swung it at the figure before her, only to find that it passed straight through it like a shadow.

"Shouldn't you be asking who I was, Eve?"

Immediately her stomach clenched cold, her legs rendered to jelly. Recognition charged through her like the knife that had left so many marks on the body she'd found lifeless on the floor. Marks that were still visible on the shape that appeared before her now.

"It can't be. I must be hallucinating. Or dying."

"I can assure you that it's neither, Eve. In life, I was your partner in everything. As children, we played together. As youths, we studied together. As young women, we dreamed of the lives we would live, our children calling one another *'auntie'* as we raised them like family. You know precisely who stands before you."

Her knees gave out from underneath her, and Eve sagged into the chair she had been sitting in only moments earlier. "Marlene. How—I found you. We buried you. How is this possible? No," she shook her head, rubbing the space between her eyebrows, attempting to clear the fog from her brain. "There must have been something terrible in that food I ordered. Food poisoning, drugs, or indigestion caused by eating it too quickly. There is more of gravy than grave about you." She waggled her finger indignantly at the specter, her denial as deep as the river the word rhymed with.

"You do not believe in me?" The ghost's expression grew even more sad than it had before.

"Of course not!" She spat out a short, harsh laugh. "One never believes the delusions formed when sitting alone in the dark."

The glowing figure appeared to have tears streaming down its pallid cheeks as it directed its gaze downward to the floorboards. After a moment, the specter raised its head in an agonizing cry, its corpselike jaw unhinging for a moment as it let out an unearthly howl. Such a wind began to blow through the house that all the open doors at once slammed shut, the curtains on the windows blew nearly off their rods, and Eve's pajamas flew off the fireplace grate and onto the floor.

Cowering in fear, Eve slid from her seat and huddled on the old threadbare rug that lay before the fireplace.

"What do you want from me, Marlene?"

The specter lifted her head and looked somberly into the face of her old friend.

"Much."

"I would give you anything you asked, dear Marlene. But what could I possibly do for you? Nothing could bring you back."

The ghost shook her head a second time, confirming Eve's lament. Indeed, nothing could bring Marlene back.

"I need you to find my killer, Eve. He has taken so much more than even you know."

Eve snapped her head up, anger lighting in her eyes.

"Of course, I know what he stole! Do you forget, Spirit, that I was the one to find your battered body? Do you realize that I washed my hands over and over just to get the feeling of your blood off of them? That I had—*have* nightmares almost every night since you died?"

"That is why this is your task, Eve. I am not the only unfortunate woman he has killed."

Eve's blood ran ice-cold. So cold, in fact, that she glanced behind her to see if the fire had extinguished in the unearthly wind moments before.

"What are you saying?"

"This man, my killer, he has killed before. Indeed, many times."

"A serial killer?" Eve thought her blood would never warm again, each new revelation bringing with it more horror than the last.

Marlene's ghost nodded slowly, her once beautiful dark hair dancing eerily about her face, which was still marred by the wounds inflicted by her attacker.

"He has gone undetected; each woman he made his victim remains either a cold case or has yet to even be discovered. He kills only once a year."

"On Christmas Eve." Eve's eyes grew round as dinner plates, grim realization dawning upon her at last. With this realization came a second, crippling one. If she had not taken a late shift at work from a friend who had children at home, she and Marlene would already have been safely tucked away at Marlene's parents' home. Marlene's death was her fault.

As if her old friend's specter could read her thoughts, she reached for Eve, but the transparent hand passed right through the solid body, leaving only an icy chill in its wake. "No, Eve. You can't think that way. He still would have found a way to do what he did." The ghost beckoned her toward the window, which swung open as she gestured to it.

"Look down into the garden below us. Each of these women cannot rest until she is vindicated—until our killer is brought to justice.

Eve stepped to the window, her eyes locked on the hand stretched out to her. A few of the fingers were bent as if the bones had been fractured, the fingernails still painted Marlene's signature cheeky red broken from her desperate fight for her life. A sob erupted in Eve's throat.

"Oh, Marlie, how I wish I had been there!"

"No, Eve."

"But I could have helped you. Maybe we both could have fought him off!"

Marlene's ghost solemnly shook her head for a third time, her hair dancing again about her face.

"No, Eve. If you'd been there, then you could help none of us now. No, you'd be one of us."

At this, Eve dared to look through the window, the glass dirty with the brown filth of London's smog. Pushing the window further open to see better, she saw close to two dozen figures on the lawn, each caught in a state of constant grief. One woman wrung her hands as she paced back and forth, her words indiscernible through her tears. Another followed a man who trudged through the icy slush, imploring him to see her, to find her body where it lay in a field not far away. Yet another woman sat leaning against the fence, wrenching at her clothes and pulling her hair in agony as she wailed for her children, who thought she had simply abandoned them on a Christmas Eve long before. Each woman's ghost bore wounds that were nearly identical to the ones that had been inflicted upon Marlene. She turned back to the transparent figure of her friend and took in the sad expression on her face.

"Please, Eve. Please help us find peace. We are bound by the heavy chains of injustice as long as our killer remains free. Free to continue adding to our numbers."

The sob in Eve's throat worked its way out, salty tears streaming down her cheeks.

"What do I do? How can I make this right?"

A sad smile appeared on the illuminated face, and Marlene's ghostly hands pulled closed first the window, then the drapes, first muffling, then silencing the sounds of the spectral cries in the garden below.

"You will be visited by three Spirits—"

"Spirits? More of them? Absolutely not, Marlene. I cannot handle any more ghosts than I have already seen tonight. No offense."

"Hear me, Eve!" Marlene's ghost spoke urgently. "Not only the peace of every woman you've seen tonight lies in the balance, but yours as well. This is your only chance."

"My only chance? For what—inner peace? I'll set up a therapy session, I promise."

Marlene's ghost shook her head again, more violently this time; her hair swishing about as if underwater.

"It is much, much more than that, Eve. The Spirits will explain everything. The first Spirit will visit you tomorrow when the bell tolls one. The second will arrive at the same time on the next night, and the third will do the same."

"*Three* more nights of ghosts? Marlene, please just give me the instructions I need to help you!"

"I cannot, Eve. That is not something I am permitted to do. You must listen to the Spirits, Eve, you must!"

Staring deeply into the eyes of her friend's specter, Eve felt an uncanny urgency to believe what the figure had to say.

"Alright," she nodded slowly. "I will wait for them. All three."

"Be strong, Eve. Everything depends on this."

"I—" the words seemed to stick in Eve's throat. "I love you, Marlene. I'm so sorry. I miss you so much."

"I love you, too, Eve. Don't forget that this wasn't your fault and that you're never alone. Don't live your life shrouded in regret." With a sad but kind smile, Marlene's figure drifted through the draped windows, presumably joining the other women's spirits outside in the cold.

Eve looked around her bedroom, feeling that it was suddenly much more vast and empty than before. She picked up the pajama set that had fallen to the floor, finding that the fabric was still warm, and changed into the soft garments. By default, she reached for her smartphone to check the time, only to be disappointed by its darkened screen. A quick glance at the antique clock on the mantle told her that it was just past two am, although she had never heard the chime. How on earth the time had passed so quickly, she did not know. Had Marlene's ghost truly been here for several hours? She turned down the thermostat on the gas fireplace, determined not to rack up too high of a bill. She would be comfortable enough beneath a few layers of covers. Hands shaking and knees weak, she climbed into her bed without even a thought toward the rest of her bedtime routine and pulled the feather duvet nearly up to her eyes. For the first time in years, Eve fell asleep as soon as her head hit the pillow.

Stave II: The First of the Three Spirits

Eve awoke with a shiver. It was terribly dark outside, which made her wonder if she had woken before the dawn or slept through the day and past the sunset. The little clock on the mantle chimed out the quarter hour, its clear tones in perfect unison with the church bells down the street, so she lay among the covers, waiting for the next hour to chime. She could have gotten out of her warm bed, padded across the cold floor, and checked the hour on the clock's face, to be sure, but the room had grown a bit more frigid since she had turned down the fireplace after her harrowing experience before falling asleep. Besides, there was something entirely terrifying about meeting a ghost that made one leery of getting back out of bed. You never knew what might be lurking beneath the bed frame, waiting to grab your ankles and pull you into some horrible depth below the floorboards.

Bah.

There was nothing beneath the bed frame. Was there? She pulled her legs up closer to the rest of her body, curling into a ball beneath the blankets.

Humbug.

Of course, there wasn't anything there. Of this, she was…not certain. To be fair, after last night, Eve wasn't certain of anything anymore. Either way, she was absolutely not getting out into the cold to check the time when she could simply wait the quarter of an hour from the safety of her bed. As time stretched further and further into a seemingly endless void, the clock's incessant ticking was her only company. The clock and her thoughts. Had she truly met Marlene's ghost? It seemed like a fever dream. Perhaps she actually did have a fever? Feeling her face and neck with the back of her hands, then her palms, she decided that she must be sick. Yes, she must be much too sick to realize how hot her body probably was and stricken with delirium as a result. Blasted takeout must have given her food poisoning. That was it, she was sure of it. Until the clock began to strike the hour.

One.

Two.

Three.

Oh, so she had only slept for one hour. Fantastic.

Four.

Five.

Six.

Where was the sunrise?

Seven.

Eight.

Nine.

Ten.

Eleven.

Twelve.

Twelve? Her head snapped to the window, wondering if the drapes were covering the glass. No, she could see the night sky between the swaths of old fabric hanging from the antique iron rod. It certainly wasn't daylight outside. Eve lay very still, pondering her spectral visit that seemed as though it had been a full twenty-four hours previously. If—and that was a very doubtful *if*—it was true, and she had indeed been visited by the spirit of her old friend, then what could she possibly do with the information that had been given to her? A serial killer? Had her friend really been just one of many innocent victims murdered by the same evil person? If that was the case, then how on earth was she going to find out who it was? Was she supposed to stop this dangerous person herself?

Distracted by her thoughts, Eve barely registered the clock when it chimed.

A quarter past the hour.

Half past the hour.

Three-quarters past the hour.

Before she knew it, the clock let out a singular, lonely chime. The chime, which should have been short and sweet, grew longer and longer, all the while growing louder and louder until she was forced to cover her ears and clench her eyelids shut, just as she'd done the night before when the butler's bells rang so hard that it seemed as if her teeth chattered in her skull. When the ringing of the chime finally died down, Eve cautiously removed her hands from the sides of her head and peeked out through squinted eyelids.

Nothing. Nothing but silence echoed through the room at long last. She heaved a sigh of relief, then pulled the duvet all the way over her head in a desperate attempt to go back to sleep.

Just as she was getting comfortable again, Eve felt a strange tugging on the bedclothes. She clenched her fingers tightly to the fabric, panic rising in her throat. No, it couldn't possibly be another specter! She must be hallucinating! Even as she told herself this, she could not be convinced. Momentarily, the covers were wrenched from her grasp and she blinked as she was confronted by a small figure that beamed with light. The light from this figure bounced off of every surface in the room, making everything bright and golden as though Eve were outside on a warm summer's day. Once her eyes had adjusted to the light, the figure before her became clear. It was short in stature, similar to a child, but with a wizened face. Much like Marlene's ghost, its hair floated through the air, glowing with the same golden light that emanated from its body, filling the room around it. While this apparition did not have the same ghoulish presence that the previous ghost had, Eve felt a chill go up her spine just the same.

"Who are you?" Her voice barely escaped her throat, the words whispering past her lips so quietly that even she herself could barely hear them.

A gentle smile formed on the face of the small being, its eyes crinkling kindly. Eve took in its entire appearance. A white dress made of many layers of lace and sheer fabrics floated gently about its little feminine body, tiny hands clasped together delicately in front of it, and small, cherub-like feet dangled in the air below the hem of the gown. At its waist was a golden cord worn like a belt, and it clutched in its grasp a lit candlestick. A sprig of green holly laden with red berries adorned its locks of hair.

"Are you the Spirit I was told would come when the clock struck one?"

"I am," the small specter nodded kindly. "Some call me *Innocence,* but I am the Ghost of Christmas Past." The small Spirit gazed kindly upon Eve as she trembled with nervous anticipation. "You have nothing to fear from me."

"You said you are the Ghost of Christmas Past," she watched the being cautiously. "Long past?"

The Spirit shook its head gently, hair swishing slowly through the air.

"No. Your past."

Indignant, Eve recoiled. Her past had already been dredged up enough for one night. For two nights, as a matter of fact.

"What concern do you have for my past?"

"Your welfare."

Eve's face must have twisted strangely at that statement, because the Spirit quickly rephrased: "Your reclamation, then. Come quickly."

Eve watched as a tiny hand reached out. "Take my hand and fly with me."

"Fly? Spirit, I am not like you. I—I'm mortal, and I'll fall!"

"Have faith, dear one, as you once did in things unseen."

If asked later, Eve would not be able to describe why she did as the Spirit instructed without any argument, but it was as if she obeyed compulsions beyond her own control. She took the Spirit's small hand, finding it warm and comforting, and they made their way to the window. In a moment, Eve realized that they were not walking, but floating, and the window pushed open before them as if by a magic breeze, revealing the streets of London below, glittering with streetlamps that crafted a miniature milky way along the aged streets of the city. With a sharp, nervous breath, she clutched the hand of the Spirit more tightly, then found herself pulled quickly into a rush of warm light. The wind blew her pajamas and hair all about her, and the light was so white that she could not see. When the wind died down and the light was no longer blinding, she opened her eyes to a familiar scene. The pair was standing in the corridor of an elementary school. Eve could smell the paste and crayons, and hear children chanting their mathematics memorization in some classroom several doors from where she stood. Christmas coloring pages and decorations made of construction paper adorned the surrounding walls, signs of the season everywhere she looked.

"I think you know this place?" The tiny Spirit looked up at her expectantly.

Eve nodded as she continued to take in her surroundings.

"It's my old school when I was a child. I haven't

been in this building in, oh…"

"Nearly fifteen years," the Spirit offered.

"Yes, I left this school not long after my parents died."

The door to one of the classrooms ahead of them stood open, and Eve tip-toed quietly in that direction. A small girl sat alone at her desk, the ones surrounding her empty. The remnants of a Christmas party were all around; a life-sized Santa Claus cutout had been taped to the wall, and confetti from Christmas crackers littered the floor. The teacher spoke into a telephone in hushed tones from where she sat at her desk. After a few moments, the woman hung up the handset and then walked to the child at the desk. Kneeling, she looked into the little girl's face and took her hand.

"Eve, darling," the woman's voice caught in her throat. "Your parents tried very hard to make it to the Christmas party today."

"Was that them on the phone?" A hopeful light came into the young Eve's eyes.

"No, it—it was the police."

"Why was it the police on the phone?" The little forehead scrunched up in concern, eyes searching her teacher's face.

"There has been an accident, sweetheart. I'm going to take you home with me tonight, alright? Would you like to play with my cat tonight?"

Confusion played on the little face, but she hesitantly nodded in agreement. Grown Eve and the Spirit watched as the little girl held tightly to her teacher's hand and the two walked from the room.

"That was the day that my parents died. They were on their way to my class's Christmas party, just like Miss Pendleton said, when a dog ran out in front of their car. Dad tried to avoid it but hit black ice on the road. Their car spun out of control. I was told that they were already gone when the police arrived, but that they were holding hands." She clenched the edge of her pajama top in her fist nervously. "Sometimes I wish I had been with them."

"They dreamed of a full life for you."

"The life I live is anything but full." Bitterness cracked the words as they left her throat.

At this confession, the Spirit lifted its candlestick high into the air, and the strange pair were whisked away to another Christmas.

Eve and the Spirit were now standing in a dark alleyway, muffled screams coming from behind the dirty glass of a dimly lit window. The Spirit extended its arm to indicate that Eve should step closer to the window.

"This is his first victim. Someone no one would probably spend much time looking for."

Turning her head sharply to look at the Spirit, Eve whispered as if she were not a specter and afraid of the killer hearing her as he worked. "A prostitute?"

The Spirit nodded sadly.

"She didn't go by her legal name, so a proper identification was never made, and without a name, the case went cold. This nameless woman now lies in a grave not far from here. Her headstone is as plain as the name they assigned to her."

"Jane Doe?"

The Spirit nodded its petite head again.

Stepping closer, Eve reluctantly peeked through the window to see the killer bent over the poor woman, his hand clutching a knife, which he then plunged into her over and over again. Eve jumped back at the shock of such a scene. She could hide neither her revulsion nor her terror at the violence on display in front of her. When the killer was sure that his horrific job was complete, he wiped his knife clean with her clothes and thrust it into his belt before stealthily leaving the residence; leaving a nightmare of epic proportions in his wake.

"After he committed this crime, his zeal for blood was unleashed."

"Why does he kill?" Eve felt her stomach curdling.

"He kills because he desires control. He was abused by his mother as a child and then abandoned before he was grown. As a result, he chooses women that he feels reflect the same characteristics of his own mother. His mother was also a prostitute, but not all of his victims lived lives such as hers. Some were drug addicts, some were dog walkers, mothers, and one even sold him coffee."

"Marlene." Eve's blood ran colder than before.

The Spirit nodded solemnly.

"Yes. He chose her simply because she had the same color hair as his mother. There is very little rhyme or reason to his choices. He simply strikes the victims that catch his attention."

Eve felt herself getting sick to her stomach again. The ground seemed to swirl beneath her feet, and her vision grew spotty and blurred. She rushed, stumbling over her own two feet, over to a small bush near a wall, emptying the contents of her stomach onto the ground. That pathetic soup and soggy bread were all she had going for her, and now she didn't even have them to depend on.

"I'm so sorry," she began to apologize, her face aflame with embarrassment as she knelt in the snow.

"Grief sometimes needs to be expelled. It is toxic when held in."

She wiped her mouth with the back of her hand, her whole body trembling in fear and disgust.

"Please show me another Christmas. One with no killing in it."

The Spirit nodded and raised its candlestick again, taking them to another December night. This one was jovial and filled with cheer.

"This Christmas doesn't seem as dismal." The Spirit prompted.

"Oh my," Eve's eyes lit up, and she stepped closer to the window that separated her from the past. "It's Miss Pendleton's wedding! Except that she's Mrs. Fezziwig now. Such a ridiculous name." She tried to sound disparaging but could not hide her delight at the event playing out before them. There was music and laughter, dancing, and food everywhere you looked. You could tell just by looking through the window that the room was filled with the warmth of bodies and mirth. The bride and groom swirled around the floor like graceful figurines on a music box, flushed pink with joy and stolen kisses.

"This woman is important to you?" The Spirit prompted.

"Y-yes, I suppose. She never stopped looking out for me, even after I graduated from her class. My case worker always made sure that Miss Pendleton was allowed to keep me on weekends and holidays."

"And now?"

Eve's reflection in the glass revealed eyes filled with regret.

"I don't go anymore. Things weren't the same after she got married. She—she didn't need me. She has a family of her own now, anyway."

"She still invites you, does she not?"

Eve shrugged, taking a step back from the window

and wrapping her arms around herself.

"It's only out of pity or obligation. Maybe both. I'm sure she's relieved that I don't go. I'm no fun at parties these days, anyway."

They watched as an eighteen-year-old Eve and Marlene stood by the punch bowl, whispering conspiratorially over their cups of punch, girlish giggles erupting, causing Marlene to nearly spit her drink on Eve. Both girls began to laugh until they had to catch their breath. A smiling young man approached the girls, asking if Eve would be his partner in the next dance, an invitation which she excitedly accepted.

"This young man seems to mean a great deal to you, as well."

Eve stepped closer to the window again, reaching for the glass that served as a barrier. She drank in the sight of him, her hand resting on the cold surface of the window in longing. Handsome in a green wool jumper and brown corduroys, he glowed with the beauty of a youth in love. He had indeed been in love with her once. And she had been in love with him.

"He did, yes."

"I see that he still does."

She glared with eyes afire at the Spirit for a moment before realizing that there were tears streaming down her face.

"Charlie was my boyfriend. We were to be married."

"Were?"

"Were. I—" She faltered. "I should have pulled him closer instead of pushing him away. I didn't want to hurt him."

The two specters stood and watched the young pair dance and twirl to the joyful music as if they had not a care in the world. With a wave of the Spirit's candlestick, they were transported yet again to a Christmas only one year later.

In a dark room, spectral Eve was forced to watch as Marlene struggled against her attacker. Eve looked on helplessly, as heartbroken now as she was on the night of the event. Unsure if the screams she heard were Marlene's or her own, Eve tried desperately to stop the killer, but her spectral hands only passed through him, never making contact—much like how Marlene's ghostly hands had passed through her body back in her room the night before. When his deed was done, she saw him wipe off his knife on Marlene's clothes, just as he had done with his first victim in the alleyway. But this time, he winced before escaping out the window of their dormitory room. Excitement waved over her as Eve realized that he'd cut himself in the struggle with Marlene. His blood must be on Marlene's clothing, mingled with hers! Eve turned to the Spirit.

"Did they ever check any of the victims' clothing for other DNA samples?"

The Spirit just shook its head in reply.

"This is why I have brought you here. To see the truths in your past. So that you might advocate for justice."

"If only I could see his face."

No sooner had she said that than spectral Marlene witnessed herself returning to the shared dorm room. She turned away from the shadow of her former self, imploring the Spirit.

"Please, Spirit, I don't think I can stomach this again."

"Very well," the Spirit nodded kindly and began to raise its candlestick. "One more Christmas to visit."

A room filled with candlelight appeared before them. It was Eve's sitting room. The rug, the armchair, the sofa, and all the decorations were hers. It appeared to be the same sitting room, but the warmth that filled it was very different from the current state of her home.

"Darling, we should settle on a date for the wedding. Things will start booking up fast, and if we want to honeymoon over university break, then we need to hurry up and plan."

"I don't think I have the heart for it anymore."

Charlie sat in the armchair in her living room, a big black cat purring happily in his lap. Eve huddled on the sofa, looking like a crumpled heap of throw blankets as she stared blankly into the fire.

"Would you rather elope? That might be more romantic, anyway."

"No, Charlie," her vacant eyes looked at him bleakly as she heaved a tired sigh. "I think you know that we can't go on like this."

He got up from his place in the armchair, leaving the cat, and knelt on the floor in front of her. Taking her small hands into his large ones, he kissed their knuckles gently.

"We can take as long as you need, Eve. I know this last year hasn't been easy on you."

"I don't need any more time, Charlie. This is over. You deserve someone who isn't so broken;" she pulled her hands from his, turning away from him to face the fire. "You deserve someone who has life left in her."

As Eve watched herself break the heart of the man she loved, her tears began to flow freely. After Marlie's death, she'd been so caught up in her own grief that she failed to see the man who was willing to stand alongside her through it all. He knelt on the floor of her sitting room, grasping her hands again and begging her not to push him away, but she drove him from her and burrowed even more deeply into her grief. In time, she would find that even her cat, Dickens, would betray her and miss Charlie so deeply that he would cry and howl at the door for hours on end. Eventually, she gave up on the animal and sent him to live permanently with Charlie. She found herself wondering if Dickens was doing alright. If he still liked to sit on Charlie's lap. A horrible thought struck her now: perhaps Dickens might also receive the attention of a new woman in Charlie's life. She watched history continue to unfold as Charlie walked dejectedly out of the room, pausing to look back at her where she sat, unmoving.

"I love you, Evelyn. I always will."

And with that, he walked out of her life, taking any spark of joy that was left with him. Spectral Eve sank to the floor of her flat, crying until she could no longer see.

"Spirit, show me no more. I can't bear it. Please, show me nothing else. Haunt me no longer!"

Head resting on her arms, she leaned forward and sobbed deep, wracking cries. When she had finally cried it all out, she tilted her head back against the wall and opened her eyes. She wasn't in her sitting room downstairs anymore, but back in her bedroom. The Spirit had gone, taking all of her strength with it. She wearily climbed to the bed and crawled back in, hoping that things would look brighter in the morning.

Stave III: The Second of the Three Spirits

With a particularly loud snore, Eve came awake with a jerk. Grumpy, and with a sleep-deprived blur to her eyes, she glared at the window. Seeing no light peeking between the curtains, she sneered in annoyance. Being forced to recall her past always put her in a terrible mood. It was one of the biggest reasons why she had never stuck with a therapist for very long. More than one counselor had told her that she needed to deal with her pain rather than allow it to fester inside of her, but it hurt too much and was more easily put back on the shelf to gather dust once more than it was to excise all the painful wounds that plagued her. After a while, she had stopped going to counselors altogether. They had all told her the same things, and she grew tired of hearing their broken records of advice that never seemed to diminish or even subdue her pain and heal her broken heart. Yet, the things she had seen over the last few hours—no, days, perhaps?—made her think more deeply about some of the things she had not known of before.

Marlene's killer…a serial killer! A disgusting villain with a long list of unnamed, uncounted victims haunted the streets of London, and the general population slept in their beds soundly, without a clue. How had this man succeeded in this kind of evil without even raising the interest of Scotland Yard? Or worse…had they simply been unable to catch him; chasing a ghost of a criminal through the streets? Her mind's eye brought back the image of that evil man as he hunched over the body of her friend. He looked thin—gaunt even. But what struck her the most was how meticulously he had cleaned his knife on her clothes. The same way that he had done with his first victim. It was clear that women meant nothing to this man. If only she had been able to get a better look at him! A shudder drove her deeper into the bedcovers until even the tip of her nose was hidden beneath them. The idea of this man lurking around any and every corner, always in the shadows, was unnerving. It became inevitable that she would not be able to fall asleep again, so for just a moment, Eve allowed herself to remember. Soon, her memory filled with blurry visions of little girls twirling in princess dresses, of pre-teens learning how to apply makeup, and of teenagers nearly grown into young women. All too soon, the hour began its habitual chime from the clock resting on the mantle, pulling Eve from her reverie. A light began to grow outside her room, shining through the crack beneath the bedroom door. It glowed slowly at first, then it strengthened in its luminosity. Frozen with fear, all the worst things her imagination could muster came to mind, torturing her already vivid imagination. After a moment, however, her curiosity got the better of her. Slowly, ever so slowly, she pushed aside the blankets and slid her feet to the floor. A new chill raised all the hairs on her legs as her feet made contact with the cold floor before she remembered to push them into her slippers. She moved through the room, carefully picking up the fire poker on her way to the door. She had left it leaning against the wing chair, too shocked after the visit from Marlene's ghost to remember to put it away. How many days had passed since Marlene's visit, anyway? That was Christmas Eve, *one*. The first Spirit had come then…on Christmas Day, *two*. So, then, this must be the day after Christmas, *three*.

Slowly, stealthily, Eve worked her way towards

the light. It was coming from downstairs, probably in her parlor. Curiosity drew her like a cat creeping around corners, and so she slunk cautiously along the edges of her room and out the door, then down the corridor, feeling safety in the nearness of the walls. Nothing could creep up on her so easily with her back to the wall. The light was warm and bright, so bright that it was as if the electricity had come back on, but the color was all wrong for that. It was more like a fire had been lit in the fireplace, but she refused to use the one in the downstairs sitting room anymore. It cost too much to run. She held her breath as she tiptoed down the steps one at a time, oh-so-gingerly. Hands growing slick with sweat, she refreshed her grip on the fire poker held aloft over her shoulder. Nearly to the step that would give her a view of the room below, she heard a voice boom out into the darkness around her.

"Come in, and know me better, woman."

Holding her breath in fear, a cold sweat broke out over Eve's entire body. Her hands shook so hard that she could barely keep her grip on her weapon.

"Come and be warmed by the fire. All your fears will I alleviate."

Wide-eyed, she continued her trek down the broad staircase until she came into full view of the illuminated room. Beside the fireplace, on a wide throne of a chair, was seated a portly old man with a white beard clothed in a red suit trimmed in fur. In his hand, he gripped a horn that was not unlike a horn of plenty. From it came a stream of blinding white light that illuminated all around it. Eve could not stare directly at it for fear of losing her eyesight, so bright was its glow. The man nodded his head slightly as she regarded him, a twinkle in his eye indeed assuaging all of her fears. As anxious as she was about this entire idea of Spirits visiting her in the night, she knew that she had nothing to dread from this one in particular.

"Come in and know me better, ma'am." He stretched out his hand invitingly, and Eve found herself reaching back. Every bit of him glowed with the pure light of the sun. His skin, his hair, and his clothes, everything shone with a shimmering gleam. It was as if he had been dusted all over with fine glitter, and the indescribable beauty of him drew her in. She felt her eyes draw to his face, scanning first the white, curled beard that hung over his chest, then his droll mouth. He smiled at her, drawing it up like a bow, and she instantly felt shame, her eyes averting to the floor.

"What do you fear?"

"Not you, gentle Spirit," Eve began to tremble. "I fear what you may reveal to me."

The large hand now came to rest comfortingly on her shoulder, and Eve was surprised by the weightlessness its presence brought to her.

"Whatever comes of this Present hour," his deep voice was smooth and velvety, reminding her of a grandfather she'd never met. "I promise to stand and face it beside you."

She finally grew the courage to look up once more. Her eyes took in the crimson of his robe, the soft rabbit fur edging, the curls of his beard, and at last the kindness of his gaze. She felt assured of her safety with this being, no matter what she might have to face.

"Who are you?"

"I am the Ghost of Christmas Present, my dear."

"I can't say that I have ever met anyone like you before, although you seem familiar to me."

"You have not met me before, that is true. However, you have met some of my brothers before me."

"Perhaps," Eve chewed her lip, struggling to remember where she had seen a person resembling this spirit before. "How many brothers do you have?"

Leaning close and winking his eye with a turn of his head, he whispered conspiratorially. "There are more than two thousand in total!"

"More than two thousand brothers? I think your parents need to learn to play cards or something."

The Spirit tipped his head back and laughed joyously; a deep, roaring laugh filled with mirth.

When he had finished unleashing his amusement, he turned his sparkling eyes to her once more. "Time and Nature bring about a new Spirit each season to do his merry work all year long. When the last bell tolls on Christmas night, that year's Spirit is released to the wild beyond, and the next one is born with the morning's dawn."

Eve pondered this for a moment, but only a moment before her thoughts were interrupted by the cheerful Spirit.

"Come now, my dear, don't hurt yourself by thinking too hard," He chuckled and stood from his chair, a chair that Eve did not recognize as ever having been in her home before. Running her hand over the upholstered arm, she felt a childlike familiarity that she could not quite stick a pin into. "Now, grab hold of my belt and we shall be off."

She reached for the wide belt that wrapped around his belly, a shining brass buckle connecting both ends of the leather. Her fingers nearly reached it when she pulled them back with a jerk, clutching them in a fist against her chest. "Where are we going?"

"We fly where the night takes us."

"*Fly?!* But, Spirit, I am mortal! What if I fall?"

"You shall not fall on the winds of Christmas, my dear. Have faith and take hold of my belt."

There was such kindness and confidence in his

voice that she knew he must be trustworthy. Reaching out once more, Eve grasped the Spirit's belt. As her fingertips touched the gleaming brass buckle, they were quickly whisked away out the window, soaring over the city of London. The buildings below them sparkled like mirror reflections of the starry skies, lights illuminating windows and streets, despite the late hour. Lovers strolled through the streets, walking hand in hand along the Thames. Delivery lorries rumbled between buildings, unloading their goods into oversized doors behind storefronts. The spectral pair picked up speed and whizzed through the air toward the horizon, which now glowed with the hues of dawn. Just as Eve was afraid that they would strike the sun and be burned to death, she found that she and the Spirit were now standing on the streets of the city, surrounded by people moving to and fro. They called to one another, wishing friends and strangers alike a Merry Christmas. Arms were laden with packages, embraces were exchanged. Smiles were traded even more often than money changed hands, and cheer was so evident that you could nearly reach out and grab it in the air, taking some for yourself. A merry trio of musicians played carols on a street corner and a small crowd had gathered to take part in the singing. It was as if Christmas was everywhere and that every*one* was Christmas.

"Where have you brought me, Spirit?"

"Do you not recognize this joyous place?" He gestured down the streets lined with colorfully painted buildings strung with twinkling fairy lights. The street lamps and every door up and down the way were festooned with jolly wreaths, and the windows boasted displays of Christmas ornaments such as tiny villages or decorated trees.

"Camden Town," she whispered the name almost to herself. "I never come here."

"Never, you say?" The Spirit was generous enough to feign surprise. "I thought you more fun-loving than all that."

"No, I used to come a lot, but I haven't been here in years." She felt someone rush past her and recognized the laughter even before she saw the laugher's face. "Babs!" She called out to her assistant, who dashed arm-in-arm with a man—Eve assumed this was Babs' beloved husband that she never shut up about—into a shop nearby.

"Do you know this woman?"

"She works for me, yes. Babs!" she called out again, louder this time, hoping to be heard.

"We are merely specters to them, my dear."

"Let's follow them." Eve ignored the Spirit's reminder and ran across the cobbled street, into the same shop door without checking to see if the Spirit was behind her. The bell jingled as she pushed open the door, but no one inside seemed to notice. She spied Babs and her husband standing in front of a display of Christmas crackers and stepped close to them.

"Do you prefer the red and green ones or the pack of golden ones?" Babs dabbed her nose, red and chapped, with a frilled hankie before stifling a cough. She was still getting over the cold she'd had all week.

The man chuckled brightly, smiling at his wife. "I like the red and green."

"Good call," Babs tucked the box under her arm. "They will look pretty with our table setting." She meandered further into the shop, her husband following close behind her. They stopped to watch displays of stuffed reindeer that stood on their hind legs, shaking their hips to a song about someone's grandmother getting run over by one of them. A raucous laugh erupted behind Eve, causing her to turn in surprise. The Spirit was wiping tears of laughter from his cheeks.

"Those Americans and their songs! As if my deer would hurt anyone's grandnan!" He continued laughing as he pressed a button on a snowman's foot, making it dance the same little jig singing *Frosty the Snowman* in a mechanical voice. Babs and her husband were moving towards a decorated tree, and Eve and the Spirit continued to follow them. Babs reached for an ornament in the shape of a rattle, stroking it wistfully. She perused several ornaments before finally plucking one from the tree's plastic branches and admiring it with tears in her eyes.

"This is the one." She held it aloft where it could catch the light. It was a tiny snow globe with a bundled-up baby sitting in a pile of fake snow, looking up as if to watch the flakes drop down from above its head. Etched into the glass was the phrase, *'Baby's First Christmas'*. "I really thought we would be using them this year," Babs whispered to her husband, a sob catching in her throat.

"I know," he whispered back, kissing her hair and drawing her close to him. "I thought this would be the Christmas when we could at last put each year's to good use."

"It seemed like we were finally going to be a family until…"

Eve gasped, a hand flying to her mouth in horror. Had Babs had a miscarriage earlier this year? She thought back, going over the year in her mind. Several months back, Babs had taken almost a week's worth of sick time, which Eve had insisted be unpaid. Had Babs lost a much-desired pregnancy and had Eve shown her unkindness during the tragic loss?

"Every Christmas for five years, Babs and Emmett have bought an ornament for the baby they hope to have. Their greatest wish is to be a family."

"Did, did Babs…"

"Lose a child? Yes. Carried for a few weeks with love, only to return to Heaven before it could even be given a name. Their world shattered, but they have love enough to find the strength to rebuild and start again."

Eve watched the couple exchange wobbly smiles and a tender kiss. "They must love one another very much."

"They do," the Spirit nodded. "If only they could share that love with a child, they would feel complete."

Babs reached to the tree again, chuckling as she touched another ornament. "Look at this one! I should get it for Eve—she never puts her laptop away."

Eve couldn't believe her ears. She stepped closer and saw that the ornament was in the shape of a laptop small enough for a doll to use. Babs was thinking of her? Buying her a gift for Christmas? Her heart began to swell. No one had thought so kindly of Eve in years!

"Why would you buy a gift for *her?*"

Emmett's sharp inquiry felt like an icy cold slap to the cheek.

"Because, Emmett, she's all alone."

"But she is mean, short with you, and pays you practically nothing. If she paid you more, maybe we could afford fertility treatments."

"I know, dear," Babs cupped her husband's cheek lovingly. "But everyone needs to be loved, and I don't think she's had that in a long time."

"She probably chased everyone in her life away, as surly as she is."

"Please don't speak ill of her, Emmett. I think she needs a friend more than she knows."

Eve turned to the specter at her shoulder. "Please, Spirit. Please tell me that they have a child yet to fill their home with laughter."

The Spirit's jolly face grew dark and somber as a dirge. "I see a box of unused baby ornaments by the fireplace, an empty stocking among them. If these shadows remain unaltered, no child's laughter will echo through their halls."

"It can't be!" Eve's tears flowed freely now as she watched the couple make their purchases at the counter, wishing the red-faced clerk a Happy Christmas.

"Why? You said yourself that there was a surplus population."

Clapping her hand over her mouth, Eve was stricken by the vileness of her words, spoken to Janine so bitterly. Was she truly such an embittered woman that she felt that way about her fellow man?

"Take hold of my belt," the Spirit raised his glowing horn again, looking much like a lighthouse on the edge of the sea. "We shall visit another Christmas."

With a flash of light, the scenery surrounding Eve and the Spirit changed. They stood in the front garden of a cozy home, snow falling softly from the sky. A picture window at the front of the house revealed a lively party within the residence. Guests danced and ate their fill. A woman in a festive red dress with a sprig of holly pinned to her shoulder appeared at the window, looking out toward the road as if she expected another guest.

"It's Miss Pendleton!" Eve cried out happily, running to the window and pressing her hands against the glass.

"Mrs Catherine Fezziwig, you mean." The Spirit corrected her kindly.

"Yes." Eve's excitement deflated just a bit. "That's her husband there, playing the fiddle." She pointed to a lanky man with a shock of graying red hair who expertly played his instrument for the party-goers. A small group of children danced around him, holding hands as they danced a little circular jig. With their red hair, she assumed that they were the Fezziwig children. Looking to the Spirit, he nodded kindly.

"The years have been kind to Catherine Fezziwig and her family. But she never forgot her favorite student."

Eve's head snapped up, her eyes making contact with the Spirit's.

"You don't mean me?"

"Of course I do, my dear. You know she expects you tonight."

"But I never attend their parties."

"She hopes for your presence, anyway."

For a few moments, Eve regretted not attending the yearly Christmas parties. She regretted shutting Mrs Fezziwig out of her life, and not remaining a part of the life of the woman who took her in and made her Christmases special after her parents died so long ago. She realized that her sorrow and loneliness also caused those same things in someone who loved her. Someone she loved very much in return. Eve found herself wishing that she could run inside the home filled with so much merriment and be a part of their family, to let Mrs Fezziwig be a mother to her again. She stared longingly into the eyes that searched for her like a mother who searched for her child and silently vowed to mend their relationship. If she ever woke up from this unending nightmare, that was. As she stood at the window, wishing away the barrier between herself and a life with others, another figure appeared beside Mrs Fezziwig.

Charlie.

"What is he doing here?"

"He attends this party every year." The Spirit replied.

Eve noted a small boy perched on his hip and felt as if she'd been kicked in the gut. Of course, he would have moved on. She told him to do just that. It should not hurt this much to see him happy, but it did.

"Are you waiting for her?" He asked the question while looking out the window, just like Mrs Fezziwig was. Eve stepped back from the window, desperate to escape his gaze and forgetting that she was invisible to his eyes.

"Of course I am." the woman turned to face him and placed a hand on his arm. "I'll never give up on her. Come to Mama, darling." She reached for the tiny boy, who let go of Charlie and launched himself at his mother. Suddenly, it became clear to Eve how much the toddler looked like her old teacher. This wasn't Charlie's child at all, and that made Eve's chest swell with a small whisper of hope.

Charlie watched the two walk away, wiggling his fingers at the toddler in a happy wave before turning back to the window. He pressed a hand against the glass and whispered, "I'll never give up on her, either."

Eve mimicked his action, wishing with everything in her that she could feel his warmth against her hand and not the frigid rift that separated them; that she could see him and tell him how very sorry she was, and that she still loved him. She felt the Spirit rest his hand against her shoulder and murmur that it was time to go, and a flash of light transported her away before she could protest.

When the blinding light had relented, Eve found that her cheeks were wet with tears. Tears that had not been shed in many years. They now stood in a darkened alleyway, barely any light illuminated the street.

"Why are we here, Spirit?"

"You will soon understand." The tone in his voice was still gentle, but a subtle change in it sent a chill up her spine. A set of high heels clicked against the street, and Eve turned to look in the direction of the sound. A scantily clad woman walked in the dim light, a cigarette in one hand, and a bottle of something in the other. Judging by her unsure steps and the brown paper bag wrapped around the bottle, Eve assumed it was probably liquor. A dark figure stepped from the shadows and reached to knock the liquor from the woman's hand as she took a drink.

"Oi! What's that about, mate?"

He stepped in front of her, brandishing a knife. Eve gasped loudly, clapping her hand to her mouth. This must be the man who took a life every Christmas Eve! This was Marlene's killer!

"You're going to talk." He growled out the words

menacingly, pressing the point of the knife against her abdomen.

"What do you want to know? I don't know anything about anything!"

That voice—it was familiar to Eve. She tried to place the woman's voice but was too distracted by the frightful scene unfolding in front of her. A scene that she was powerless to stop. The terrified woman was pushed down and forced onto her back, the knife still pointed at her middle. Eve could hear her pitiful cries for mercy as she begged for her life, offering her belongings, her money, and even her body in exchange for release from his threatening grip. Eve cried along with her, knowing that this was probably what Marlene's death had looked like, and she was angry to be powerless to stop yet another girl from being butchered. The killer leaned close, murmuring into the woman's ear. After a moment, she murmured a response. He let out a sinister laugh, then drew his knife into the air and plunged it into her body over and over again until her screams fell silent. He wiped the knife on her clothes and stood— a menacing and shadowy figure against the light of the lone flickering street lamp.

"Thank you." Pocketing his weapon, the man disappeared into the darkness.

Eve didn't know when she had moved to kneel at the woman's side, but even if she had not been a specter and could have performed resuscitation, it would have been too late. The most recent victim of the Christmas Killer was dead, and no one could bring her back. She steeled her nerves, willing herself to look into the woman's face. Recognition charged through her like a lightning bolt. The voice that had sounded so familiar belonged to Darla, one of the girls who lived in her dormitory at university! How had such a promising and dedicated student become a woman who worked the streets? Eve cried loudly, her heart feeling as if it had been torn from her chest. She longed to take the limp hand into her own, bringing it to rest against her cheek. She mourned for poor Darla, reduced to a wretched existence. She mourned for Marlene. She mourned not just for her friends, but for all the women that this man had murdered in cold blood. How could she help them if she didn't know who he was? Footsteps crunched in the snow beside her, and she turned her head in their direction.

"Is there no way that I can save her?"

"'Are there no prisons?'"

"*What* did you say?!" Eve was on her feet, fury pounding in her chest.

"'Is it not better that the surplus population is decreased?' Those are your words, are they not?"

Eve crumpled to the cold snow again, face to face with her own cruelty spoken to Janine before all of this horror began. The Spirit knelt beside her, laying a hand on her shoulder once more.

"This sad, fallen woman represents Want and Ignorance, and that those things often make lovely people, even intelligent ones, fall prey to all sorts of terrible things. The killer you are hunting demonstrates that best of all."

"What can I do to stop him?"

As the words left her mouth, the bells in a nearby steeple began to ring.

One.

"My time grows short, my dear. In fact, my time is at an end."

Two.

Three.

"No! I need your help!"

Four.

"That is for the next Spirit to give." The Spirit was fading from view, his face kind and compassionate as he gazed at her.

Five.

Six.

"Don't leave me, Spirit!" Her voice sounded like that of a frightened child, and not like that of a grown woman.

Seven.

Eight.

"Honor the Spirit of Christmas in your heart,"

Nine.

"and keep it all the year through."

Ten.

Eleven.

"I will try, Spirit, but I don't know how,"

Twelve.

"I don't know how."

With the last gong of the bells, all that was left of the Spirit was an ethereal shimmer that blew away in the wind.

Stave IV: The Last of the Spirits

Eve knelt in the snow beside Darla's body, unwilling to leave the deceased woman alone. When she had cried all she could, Eve opened her eyes to see that Darla was no longer on the ground in front of her. Shocked by the sudden change, she jumped to her feet, scanning the area for signs of Darla, but finding none. She didn't even see footprints in the snow left by the killer. Her breaths came in quick succession, each one more shallow than the last until it felt like her head was swimming. Why had there been so much death in her life? She had witnessed far too much brutality for one person to bear. That counseling session she had been so against really sounded beneficial at the moment. Head still spinning, she turned around. Her eyes landed on a figure shrouded in black. Tall and imposing, he wore a leather jacket and a fedora pulled down over his face. He reminded her of a menacing Indiana Jones, and if she had been taken aback or frightened by the many other specters had already encountered, she was fully terrified of this Spirit, who seemed to be Death itself. It took every fiber of her being to find the strength to form a few simple words.

"Are you the last of the three Spirits whose coming was foretold to me?"

The hat covering the face nodded slowly.

"Have I reason to fear you?"

The others had assured her they were not to be feared, but instinct told her that this Spirit would answer otherwise, and indeed he did with another slow nod of his head. An eerie mist danced about his feet, like darkened fog from an evil and icy place that reduced the temperature of anything it permeated.

"Then, take me where you will," her voice trembled so much that her words were barely audible.

With a gust of freezing wind that sucked the breath from her lungs, the shadowy mist enveloped Eve and Spirit both. When it began to fall to the ground once more, Eve saw that they were in a cold gray room, lit by unforgiving overhead lights. Two men dressed in scrubs were covering a body with a white sheet, their words muffled slightly by the masks covering their faces.

"It's always a pity to see a pretty lady taken down like this. Did you hear anything about who they might suspect?"

"No," the second man began to strip off his gloves, balling them up and tossing them in the bin as if he were playing a game of basketball. "But wounds like this definitely mean it's personal. Lookit all of 'em, Jones. Fifty-three stab wounds to the chest! There's nothing much left for the undertaker to work with."

Had the killer really stabbed Darla so many times? Eve didn't think it had been as many as that—not even close, but perhaps the trauma of it was clouding her judgment.

Jones, or Doctor Jones, as Eve realized, pulled the sheet up to cover the grisly sight. She was glad that she stood far enough away that she could not see poor Darla's features. He paused before he covered the woman's face, regarding her kindly.

"At least he didn't touch her face. Her family will have something less terrifying to say their goodbyes to."

The second doctor was now removing his mask and the paper gown that he wore over his scrubs.

"I'm sure the undertaker will use too much rouge and scar the family well enough." He chuckled at his own joke, then tried to toss his full face mask into the trash bin, letting out a disappointed expletive when it fluttered to the floor instead. Next, he balled up the paper gown and aimed carefully, taking a few more seconds to ensure success. He threw the disposable garment with practiced accuracy, pumping his fist in a victory dance entirely inappropriate for a workplace such as his.

"Really, Dilber?" Doctor Jones's tone belied irritation as he kindly finished pulling the sheet over Darla's face.

"I'm headed to lunch. Don't have too much fun while I'm gone." Doctor Dilber swung the door open and whistled a jaunty tune as he exited the room. Eve hoped he choked on his beans and toast. She was appalled at the asinine way in which he had regarded her old friend.

Decrease the surplus population.

Eve shuddered at the memory of her own vulgar words. She could never, would never be that woman again. Not after the things she had seen in the company of these Spirits.

A telephone hanging on the wall began to ring, taking Doctor Jones away from his duties of tending to Darla.

"Mortuary," he answered in a clipped, professional tone. "Yes, send them down. Thank you." Hanging up the phone, he walked back to the table where Darla lay beneath the plain white sheet. "Someone that loves you has come to identify you, my dear."

Eve had never met any of Darla's family, but she remembered that the woman had several sisters and that her parents lived in a small house somewhere in the country. At least one of them must live in London to be able to arrive so quickly. In just a moment, a mechanical buzz sounded at the door, and Doctor Jones walked over to admit Darla's next of kin. He held the door open as a couple walked in. *Babs?* Babs was one of Darla's sisters? Her assistant's face was puffy with signs of recent tears. The poor woman had lost a baby and a sister all in one year. How tragic. Just one more reminder of the fragility of life. The three stood by the cold steel table where Darla lay, and Eve stepped closer. She had to say goodbye to Darla, too.

"Are you ready?" Doctor Jones' tone was kind when he addressed Babs. Emmett put his arms around his wife, offering her unfailing support. Babs nodded haltingly, fresh tears coming down her cheeks. The medical examiner gently folded the sheet down to expose only the victim's face and not anything more disturbing. Babs nodded fiercely before sobbing into her husband's chest. It wasn't Darla lying there at all.

It was Eve's body on the mortuary table.

Eve reeled out of control, feeling as if she'd been hit

by a massive lorry and plunged into an icy river all at once. How was it possible that she was staring down at herself, presumably killed by the same villain that had now murdered two of her friends? Panic rose in her throat, and she was barely conscious of Emmett and Doctor Jones discussing her body's release to an undertaker for her funeral. Of course, Babs would have to make the arrangements. Eve had no family left to speak of. Her breath came in shallow gasps, her lungs tight and squeezed as if there was a pair of hands surrounding them, pressing all the air from her chest. The cold mist that had never quite left the room enveloped Eve and the Spirit once more until the scene in front of her was only an abominable memory. When the mist again receded, lying at her feet like a menacing guard dog, she became aware that they now stood in a graveyard. Under a small tree devoid of leaves, Babs and Emmett stood before a tiny stone engraved with the words, *"Our Beloved Angels"*. Beneath those words were two consecutive years, the first of which Eve now knew was the year Babs had a miscarriage. She turned to the darkly clad Spirit, tears running down her face.

"Babs lost another baby?"

A solemn nod.

She turned back to look at the woman she should have been a friend to, but had treated like a servant. The grief and finality displayed in the couple's hunched shoulders were crippling. Facing the Spirit again, she implored him, although she was afraid that she knew the answer in her heart.

"Will they ever have children to hold?"

The Spirit shook his head slowly.

"Can't it be helped? Aren't there doctors that could do something?"

He nodded again. Realization dawned on Eve.

"They can't afford those kinds of doctors, can they?"

An even slower shake of the Spirit's head gave Eve the devastating answer she was looking for. She watched Babs and Emmett walk up a small hill to a freshly dug grave where a small group was gathered. Eve and the Spirit followed them, the deathly mist now clinging to her ankles with every step, working its way ever slowly up her legs as if it sought to devour her. She drew close enough to realize that this gathering was comprised of people who had once loved her. Perhaps they loved her still. Standing among Babs and Emmett, listening to the words of a clergyman, were Mr and Mrs Fezziwig and Charlie. Charlie. Eve clutched her chest at the sight of him. How she loved him still! If only she could be assured that she had not destroyed his life when she had certainly destroyed her own!

"Spirit, please tell me that he finds happiness. I'll even be alright if he loves another. I just want him to be happy if I can't be with him."

The Spirit shook his head in response. A loud groan escaped Eve's throat, the pain she had kept bottled up for so long now escaping anew. She ran to Charlie's side, barely noticing the departure of her precious few other mourners. He was bending close to the stone already inscribed with her name. She knelt in front of him, imploring him to see her.

"Please, Charlie! I'm here, please see me!" She grasped for his face, her spectral hands passing straight through him instead of caressing him as she hoped. "Charlie, please...I love you!" Sobs overtook her, and she continued to reach for him, her every attempt unsuccessful. All too soon, he laid a single red rose against the stone inscribed with her name. He brought trembling fingers to his lips, kissing them softly before pressing their tips to her name. Her name was just as cold as her body was beneath the soil. Eve watched helplessly as the only man she'd ever loved walked sadly away from the graveyard. His shoulders hunched, head hung low, headed for a life filled with more sadness than any man could deserve. Eve hugged her knees, rocking back and forth as she sobbed. She cried for the man she loved. She cried for the time they lost when she drove him away. She cried for the future they would never have if this fate came to pass. All her tears unshed over so much loss came in a flood that could not be controlled.

Feet crunching on the snow interrupted her tears.

"Charlie?" She looked up, expecting to see her beloved returning, and was shocked to see another face bending down to look at her gravestone, putting him nearly eye to eye with Eve.

Derek Miller. What was he doing at her funeral? He had been a regular at the coffee shop where Marlene had worked. He hit on a lot of girls, including Marlene, but he was a creep and none of them would go out with him.

"It's good to see you again. I haven't seen you since I was at your house on Christmas Eve. Too bad I couldn't take another look at what I did to you that night."

Eve scrambled backward until she bumped into the cold granite. A silent scream lodged in her throat. Derek must have been her killer! He picked up the rose that Charlie had given to her, regarding it with a sinister sneer.

"Put that down! That belongs to me!" If only someone could hear her. Had anyone heard her at all when he stabbed her to death?

"I never thought I'd find you." he twirled the rose between his fingers before brushing it seductively against his lips. "It was supposed to be both of you that night—you and your friend. What was her name? Marlene? That little tease that sold me coffee every day. She wanted me so bad. But you were in the way. Always hanging around and distracting her. You were supposed to be there when I came to your dorm room. It took me seven years to find out who you were. I tracked down that whore Darla last year, and she gave me your name. Eight long years. I finally made you mine." he ripped the velvety petals from the stem, crushing them in his fist. "Now you are mine forever. Thanks for the locket, by the way." He dropped the bruised and ripped petals onto the overturned dirt with an evil grin and stood to walk away.

Eve clutched at her pajama shirt, finding that the silver locket engraved with holly and berries no longer rested securely against her collarbone. A Christmas gift from her parents that she and Mrs Fezziwig had found placed beneath the Christmas tree the year her parents died. Inside, they had engraved a message and put a tiny picture of their family. Eve wore it every single day and only took it off when she bathed. He must have taken it as a token of his evil deed. Realization dawned like a bright new day. If he took a token from her murder, then he probably took tokens from the other women as well. This could be the key to everything. Turning to the Spirit, Eve's fervent begging changed from one of despair to one of desperate hope.

"Spirit, please tell me that I have another chance.

That I can make things right! I will do everything I can to bring Derek Miller to justice and to help everyone he harmed find peace! Please tell me that I can succeed, and wipe my name from this stone! I promise not only to fight for these women, but to live my life as I should, and to show love to mankind. I promise to honour Christmas in my heart and try to keep it all the year. I will live in the Past, the Present, and the Future. The Spirits of all three will live within me. I will not shut out the lessons that they teach, and I will treat my fellow man with kindness and dignity."

No longer afraid of the otherworldly specter of Death, she clutched his legs in supplication. Tears streamed down her cheeks yet again, accompanying her pleas for more time. For a second chance. For justice for those who could no longer seek it for themselves.

Stave V: The End of It

E ve awakened in a cold sweat, clutching her pillow as if it were the legs of the third and final Spirit. She looked about her room, finding everything in its place. Her bed was as it had always been, and the fireplace was lit once again. She ran to the wall and flicked on the lights, only to find that her electricity was still out. Laughing maniacally, she flipped the switch off and on again several times in a row. She reached for her throat and grasped at her locket, reassured to find it once again fastened around her neck where it ought to be.

"I don't know what to do," she amazed aloud. "I feel as giddy as a schoolgirl. As light as a feather." She ran wildly back to her bed and scrambled to stand on the soft surface. She began jumping up and down on the mattress, knocking all of her pillows and half of her comforter to the floor in her glee. "If Marlene were here, I'd start a merry pillow fight with feathers everywhere!" Eve began laughing heartily to herself at the memory of the two little girls and their childhood pillow fights, their mothers only half scolding them for jumping on the beds. If anyone saw her at the moment, they would probably imagine her a drunkard, such was her grand and intense merriment. Out of breath, she sat down among the coverlet, then slid to the floor, resting against the bed frame. She closed her eyes, smiling as her breath steadied. This was real. She was in her home, her room. How long had she been gone? Her room was brightening, so she rushed to the window and threw the curtains back, instantly blinded by the light now streaming in. The streets were lined with the same dirty snow drifts that she had seen the night before, and a handful of people walked up and down the pavement on their way to various destinations. Looking down at the pedestrians, she saw the same delivery boy who had dropped her soup on Christmas Eve among them. She flung open the window, calling down to him.

"You, there!"

The teenager nearly dropped the takeout boxes of Chinese food that he was carrying. Recognizing the house and her voice from before, he visibly tensed.

"Yes, ma'am, can I help you?"

"What day is it?"

"Pardon?" He looked as if he thought her bonkers.

"The day, the month, the year. What day is it today?"

"It's Christmas Day, lady. It's almost noon on Christmas Day."

Eve gasped, her hand covering her mouth with a hollow *wop*. "They did it all in one night! The blessed Spirits did it all in one night!" She danced a little jig, during which the delivery boy stared up at her in disturbed disbelief.

"Sure, lady. Merry Christmas."

"Wait! Please, wait just a moment!" She rushed to her purse and pulled out a thick wad of cash, not bothering to count it. She stuffed it into an empty zippered bag that had come with a makeup purchase. She tossed it down to him. "I'm sorry for my brusqueness last night. I was having a bad day and took it out on you. My sincere apologies."

The boy picked up the bag and opened it. When he saw the amount of money she had given him, his face snapped back up to look at her, shock written on his features. "Th-thank you, ma'am. That is terribly kind of you."

"Merry Christmas, my dear. May God bless you."

The boy nodded silently before using his sleeve to wipe a few tears from his cheek. "And you, ma'am.

And you. Happy Christmas!" He waved joyfully and was on his way. Eve smiled, waving until he was nearly out of sight.

It was very nearly noon, the delivery boy had said, so Eve haphazardly got dressed, shoving her feet into thick socks and galoshes to protect her feet from the London slush. She threw her dead phone and a charger into her purse, and rushed to the police station—she had a wrong to bring to justice.

Pulling open the door, Eve stepped inside the warm building. It was dingy and old, with ornaments and garland hung across the front desk that matched the overall feel of the building. An overweight officer sat leaning back in a chair behind the desk, a wide slice of mince pie on a paper plate in front of him. He sat forward; the chair creaking precariously beneath his weight.

"How can I help ya, love?"

"My name is Evelyn Scrooby. I'd like to speak to a detective, if I may."

"Of course, my dear. Let me see if someone is available to talk to ya." He picked up the phone receiver and dialed an extension number. He studied her while he waited for an answer. "Are you alright, Miss Scrooby?"

Eve smiled in response. "I am, thank you. For the first time in a long time, I'll be alright."

The officer nodded his balding head kindly, as if he understood what she meant. He spoke into the phone for a moment before hanging it up. "Detective Hallow will see you just down the corridor. His name is on the door." He pointed a rather large finger, indicating the direction she should go. "I hope you have a Happy Christmas, my dear."

Eve smiled at him again. "Thank you, I hope you do, too," she turned to walk in the direction he'd pointed in before she remembered her phone. "Could I possibly ask you to plug in my phone somewhere?" She sheepishly pulled the items from her purse and held them out. "My electricity has been out all night and I don't have a way to charge it."

The man smiled and held out a large paw for her phone and charging cord.

"Of course I will, love."

The short walk down the passage felt like the longest one she had ever taken. Her palms grew damp with sweat, her chest tight with nervous energy. She paused in front of the door, eyes fixed on the narrow black placard where the words *Det. T. Hallow* were engraved in a brassy color. She closed her eyes and focused on a few breaths, breathing into her nose and blowing out from trembling lips.

In.

Out.

In.

Out.

Lather.

Rinse.

Repeat.

With each measured inhale and exhale, Eve felt less shaky and more confident. She finally had something that could bring her best friend and so many other women the justice they deserved. The closure their families craved. The fact that her own life was at stake was not even something she remembered in that moment, so narrow was her focus and desire for justice. Eyes still closed, she wiped a sweaty palm on her pant leg and raised it to knock on the door. A sudden *whoosh* of air swept her face, her eyes popping open in surprise, fist still poised for knocking.

"Evelyn Scrooby?"

She lowered her fist awkwardly, clutching the strap of her purse with it instead. The gruff voice did nothing to continue her efforts to calm herself; instead, they drove her usual confidence even further from her grasp. Her chin led the rest of her head in a series of small nods while her tongue gathered the courage to respond.

"Yes, sir. But you can call me Eve."

He nodded brusquely, opening the door wider, gesturing to invite her into the room. He was tall, thin, and wiry, and his closely cropped hair and beard were peppered with gray—evidence of a long and stressful career. Stepping inside, she noticed that the room was filled with stacks and stacks of files. They covered nearly every surface available, from the tops of metal filing cabinets to most of his desk. There were even stacks on the floor around his workspace. He moved to pick up a stack from the chair that sat opposite his desk.

"Sorry about that. You can sit here."

Before Eve could sit, her eyes settled on a dark leather bomber jacket draped over the back of his office chair. On yet another stack of files piled on top of a cabinet in the corner of the room was a black fedora. A chill coursed through her body that felt like the terrifying mist that had accompanied the third Spirit the night before. An even deeper chill overtook her as she realized that Detective T. Hallow was dressed in the same manner as that Spirit, as well. His gruff tone was the missing piece that completed the terrifying specter. She sat down timidly, her purse held awkwardly in her lap like an old woman waiting for a bus to arrive. She watched nervously as the detective sat wearily into the old wooden chair, its springs squeaking in protest when he leaned back. He watched her with an unreadable expression for a moment before speaking.

"What can I do for you, Miss Scrooby? It must be

important to take time away from your Christmas merry-making."

"I don't make merry on Christmas, sir. Not anymore, at least. I've come because I think I've remembered a very important detail about the murder of my friend."

The chair's springs protested a second time as the detective leaned forward, resting his elbows on the worn desk between them. He tented his fingers, setting his chin on their tips as he listened more closely.

"Marlene Jacobs was my best friend." Eve closed her eyes for a moment, steeling herself. She recalled the ghostly image of her friend standing before her as it begged for help. She remembered the many women whose tortured spirits had stood around her front garden, crying for justice. Begging to be allowed to rest in peace. She found that their faces strengthened her, giving steadiness and confidence to her voice once more. "She was murdered seven years ago and her killer has never been found. Every Christmas Eve, I lie awake, haunted—tortured by the memory of finding her on the floor of our dorm room. But last night I remembered something that I had not ever recalled before."

Detective Hallow's dark eyes glinted with cautioned interest. He nodded, indicating that he was listening and that she should proceed.

"Back then, the officers who interviewed me asked over and over again if I could think of anyone who would be angry with Marlene, but she was so kind to everyone that I kept telling them she had no enemies. When we had her funeral, hundreds of people showed up to mourn her. She was truly one of the kindest people I have ever known. But last night I remembered someone else. There was a guy who often came into the coffee shop where Marlene worked. He would hit on the girls who worked there, as well as some of the regulars, Marlene included. She would complain to me all the time that he creeped her out and made her feel really uncomfortable. I was studying at the coffee shop one day about a week before Christmas when he started hitting on her pretty aggressively. I spoke up and told him that she wasn't interested, and to leave her alone. Our interaction wasn't anything noteworthy, and he just got up and left. We didn't see him again after that. But after the Christmas holiday, he completely disappeared. No one saw him around campus anymore, and I never thought about him again. But I remembered him last night, and now I can't shake it." She blew out a breath, relieved to have said her piece.

The detective tapped his fingertips together thoughtfully before leaning back in his chair again. He crossed his arms over his chest and scrubbed his short beard with a hand; the action making a bristly sound louder than Eve would have expected. She wondered if he would take her seriously, or if he would dismiss her. After a moment, he studied her again.

"Do you remember the bloke's name?"

She gathered all her courage, took a deep breath, and looked into his eyes for the first time. She had never seen the face of the third Spirit, but the eyes of this gruff man that resembled him were warm and kind. The Spirit had terrified every cell in her body, but the eyes of this detective told her that she had nothing to fear from his gruff exterior.

"Yes, his name was Derek Miller."

Detective Hallow scooted forward and reached for the mouse resting on a worn neoprene pad that had a photograph of a smiling family posing on the beach printed on it. The sentiment, "Happy Father's Day" in a faded golden typeface, was positioned along the sand at their feet. He jiggled the mouse, waking the computer screen on the desk. He began to type a series of commands into a program and then clicked a button with the mouse. After a few agonizing moments, he started to scan through the results.

"You said this was seven years ago?"

"Yes, seven years yesterday."

"And the nature of the murder?"

"Stabbing." Eve felt her eyes and throat prickle

with tears, making it difficult to get the word out.

The detective looked at her kindly. "I'm sorry for your loss," he regarded her closely. "The file here says you were the one who found her?"

She could only nod in confirmation.

More typing.

"There have been several harassment complaints filed against one Derek Miller over the years, some from the university, others from the general area. Can you give me a brief description of the man as you remember him?"

Eve closed her eyes and recalled every detail that she could, which was particularly easy since she had seen him in her strange encounter the night before. Detective Hallow nodded solemnly as she spoke, then turned his computer screen to face her. A mugshot was enlarged, taking up most of the screen. The name Derek Miller was listed ahead of a list of complaints filed against him. Evil eyes filled with darkness stared at her, the image giving her a chill.

"That's him." Her voice came out shakier than she anticipated.

He turned the screen back around and clicked around a few documents. "This mugshot is from an arrest for being a Peeping Tom, but there are no violent charges. Just a lot of complaints. It looks like he still lives a few blocks from the university where your friend was killed, as do a lot of the women who filed complaints. I'd like to bring him in for questioning."

"I have another question, sir," Eve paused, waiting for his permission. He watched her, nodding for her to continue. "I remember the officers saying that there was a bloodstain on her clothes that didn't make sense. Could he have cleaned his weapon with her clothing?"

He scrubbed his beard again, clicking through images before stopping at one and turning his head back and forth as he regarded it. "Would you be alright if I showed you a photo of her clothing?"

"Yes, sir." The memories were indelible in her mind, anyway. He turned the screen to face her again, and an image of Marlene's flowered shirt with a large smear of blood was pulled up. Remembering the scene she witnessed alongside the first Spirit, she nodded. "Yes, that is the stain I was talking about. Do you know if it, or any of her clothes, were ever tested for other DNA?"

He pecked at the keyboard, then clicked the screen a few more times.

"No, there were no signs of sexual assault, so no samples were taken. I'm going to look into this further, Miss Scrooby. In fact, I'll make it my top priority and work on this today." He stood up, and Eve followed suit. "Thank you for the tips. I will be in touch soon." He reached across the desk, extending his hand towards her.

Eve took the outstretched hand, finding herself surprised when it was warm and not cold, like the mist that accompanied the Spirit he so resembled.

"Thank you for your time, Detective Hallow. I appreciate it more than you know."

Eve hailed a taxi and headed straight for Camden Town. Her objective was singular: gifts and rich foods to contribute to the merriment at the Fezziwig home. The beautifully hand-painted card she received each Christmas not only invited her to the annual Christmas Eve party but also their home on Christmas Day. This year she would finally accept their gracious invitation. She rushed into the first shop that appeared to cater to children, its walls lined with shelves that boasted colorful displays of gifts. How many children did Mrs Fezziwig have now? Perhaps three? No, the little boy she had seen in the window made four. She purchased dolls and play makeup, tea sets, and stuffed animals. She bought little toy cars, sets of building blocks, and a stuffed dinosaur with a toothy grin that she could envision the tiny toddler hugging tightly. She bought enough books for a small library, careful to choose things that she hoped each child would love. In a music shop down the way, Eve purchased items to clean and care for Mr Fezziwig's violin and a voucher for anything else he might need. At the register, she saw a lovely songbook of carols as they would have been played during Dickens' Christmas. She picked it up and flipped through a few pages, finding a high-quality vellum aged to a lovely patina as if it were indeed kissed by the passage of time.

"The sheet music in that is period-accurate. Not one of those fly-by-night books that just looks pretty." The shopkeeper looked kindly at her over his spectacles as he rang up the rest of her purchase.

She relished the feel of the pages, closing the book and admiring the leather cover embossed with golden trim. It felt like holding a piece of history in her hands. Smiling to herself, she handed the book to the shop-keep. She extended her smile to him, as well.

"The man I'm buying for is a professor of history, so I think this is just the thing to finish out his gift."

"It's an excellent choice, ma'am. I think you'll have made his Christmas quite merry."

He finished ringing up her order and gave her the total. Still smiling, Eve tapped her card against the payment terminal and added the bags to the ever-growing bunch of them she had slung over her arms. A shop across the lane had displayed several shopping trolleys for sale on the pavement in front of their door. She recognized it as the same shop where Babs and Emmett had purchased Christmas baubles previously. Looking up and down the street, Eve checked carefully for signs of her assistant. The last thing she wanted to do was run into the couple and spoil Christmas surprises. At the door of the shop, she picked a colorful trolley in shades befitting the season and loaded her packages into it, chuckling at the idea of toting it home like an old woman. She did her due diligence as she entered the shop, checking for Babs among the other Christmas Day shoppers and finding that their paths would not yet cross. She dragged the trolley into the store and asked the clerk if she could leave it at the counter, explaining that it would be part of her purchase. The red-cheeked woman smiled merrily and let out a chortle, saying that she'd sold more trolleys that morning than all the Christmas season and that she would be happy to keep it at the counter while Eve shopped. Thanking her, Eve picked up a woven shopping basket painted with the shop's name and hung it in the crook of her elbow. Making a beeline to the display tree that was filled with children's ornaments, she carefully picked one for each of the Fezziwig children, using their mother's social media account to discern what each child might be interested in, whispering a prayer of thanks that the kind officer at the desk had charged her phone a bit while she spoke with Detective Hallow. A sugar plum fairy for the oldest, who danced in her first recital this holiday season, sweet little pencils that read, "My First Year of School" for the twins, who were five years old, and a dinosaur dressed as Father Christmas for the toddler, who seemed to wear a dinosaur tee-shirt in every photo she saw. Browsing through other display trees, she picked another ornament that looked like sheet music for "The First Noel" for their father, and a "World's Best Teacher" ornament for their mother. Her next ornament was a tiny bedazzled cellphone for Babs that seemed to match her assistant's exuberant personality. Eve moved on to the large ceramic Christmas village on display. When she was young, her teacher had collected old pieces at charity shops. Eve had loved going on hunts for them alongside her, then helping her to set up the village on a table in her sitting room. Looking at the charming village, a piece caught her eye. An old Victorian schoolhouse that looked like the one Ebenezer Scrooge might have attended was nestled in the fluffy cotton "snow" that blanketed the ceramic buildings. A smile spread across her face to see it, but a tear sprang to her eye as she spied a tiny woman and girl holding hands, walking toward the schoolhouse. The perfect gift for the woman who had taught her so many things, and felt like a mother when she had lost her own. Picking up the boxes that contained the items she chose and adding them to her shopping basket, Eve headed back up to the counter. With her smartphone pulled up for correct spellings, she asked the woman to write the name of each recipient on their respective ornaments. She kept a wary eye out for her assistant all the while, careful not to be caught in the joyful shop. When her purchases were complete, Eve thanked the clerk heartily and made her way down the street to finish her shopping, her shiny new trolley rolling smartly down the pavement behind her. Stopping at the corner, she spied an old man carving pieces of wood. In his hands was a shape that made her stop and stare in awe. It was perfect for the last person on her list.

Back at home, surrounded by more gifts than she had ever purchased, Eve hummed along with Bing Crosby's Christmas album on her phone, recharged by a battery pack purchased on her shopping spree. Remembering the phone call she had handled so unkindly the day before, she picked up her phone and started a text message to the last number that Babs had patched through.

Happy Christmas, Janine, this is Eve Scrooby.

I didn't want to call and interrupt your holiday, but I did want to reach out and apologize for my behavior yesterday. I always struggle this time of year, and I took my feelings out on you. I hope that you can forgive me. I'd like to make it up to you and make a sizable donation to the cause you mentioned. After thinking

*over what you said, I realized that you were spot on—
it is a very, very worthy cause, and you were right to
ask me to donate. I would be pleased to help out. My
assistant will be reaching out to you in the new year to
find out where to send the funds. Again, I'm really sorry
about yesterday. I hope you and James have a wonderful
holiday.*

Love, Eve

She hit *send* and set her phone back down. After
a moment or two, Eve's screen lit up again, the
familiar *ding* signaling the arrival of a text message.
She cautiously picked up the device with a nervous
cringe, hoping that it wasn't a message telling her to
get lost. She tapped the notification and opened the
new message.

*Happy Christmas to you, too, Eve! Please, don't think
anything of it. I reached out for the first time in years
without considering finding out how you were doing first.
If I had known that you were not doing well, I would
have reached out years ago and asked you to have dinner,
or at the very least, to tea. I'd love to reconnect, though!
Thank you so much for reaching back out. I hope that
you have a wonderful day with the ones you love! Let's
get tea/coffee one day next week if you're free? Xoxo,
Janine*

*P.S. Thank you for the donation in spite of my
thoughtless request!*

Eve smiled as she read the reply and quickly

pecked out a return text that she would love to meet up the next week, and promised that she would put a reminder into her phone to reach out. When she had finished scheduling the task in her calendar, she laid her phone down on the rug again and began tackling her work, wrapping the mountain of gifts she had brought home from the shops. Deciding that she needed a glass of wine to go with her merry wrapping, she went to the kitchen. Opening her refrigerator, she was thankful for the fact that she never kept much food inside of it and chose to order in for most meals. There wasn't much beyond a box of bicarbonate and a half-empty bottle of white wine. She took the wine out of the fridge, noting that it was not very cool anymore, but still cool enough to be refreshing. She poured a glass and returned to the sitting room to resume her work. After twenty minutes or so of cutting, taping, and labeling, a knock at the door interrupted her newfound hobby, prompting her to lay down her cello tape and scissors to answer the door. Upon opening, she found Detective Hallow standing on her stoop, nervously turning his black fedora in circles with his hands.

"Merry Christmas yet again, Detective. What can I do for you?"

"Happy Christmas, Miss Scrooby. I wonder if I might have a moment of your time?"

Opening the door wide, Eve welcomed him in with a smile.

She showed him to a plush chair by the fire, explaining with a laugh that her electricity had gone out the night before and she was sorry that he had to settle for firelight and sunshine through the windows.

"I'm sorry to hear that. Were you not able to get someone out to fix it last night or today?"

She waved dismissively. "No need to bother anyone on Christmas. Tomorrow will do just fine."

He cocked his head to the side, thinking for a moment. He scrubbed his hand on his beard the same way he'd done at the police station that morning.

"I wonder if you might show me to your electric panel? Perhaps a breaker has flipped."

A flipped breaker was something that Eve had not considered the night before, but it wasn't something she knew how to check, either. She took him down a dark corridor to a closet at the back of the kitchen. The old house navigated like a Victorian maze of sorts. Once they had stepped inside and the panel was illuminated by the flashlight on Eve's phone, Detective Hallow let out a happy *"aha!"* He flipped a breaker and reached for the switch on the wall— immediately surrounding them with light. Eve did a happy little dance and hugged him tightly, surprising both of them. Going back to the kitchen, Eve put a kettle on the stove for tea before inviting the detective to sit at the table while they waited.

"What brings you over here, sir?"

The detective smiled, his face more at ease than it had been when she last sat opposite him.

"Well, we went to Mr Miller's flat to try to speak with him, but he wasn't home. However, his land-lady came to her door when she heard us knocking in the corridor. We asked if she had seen him lately, and she told us that she had not seen him in a while, although she had heard him leave and return the night previously. She unlocked the door and told us to look at whatever we liked. She had several complaints filed against him from other tenants and felt that he was up to no good."

Eve's breath began to speed up, her blood pumping in her ears.

"Did you find anything?"

"Miss Scrooby," he leaned forward on the table, his hands splayed widely on the wooden surface. "We found *everything.*"

The detective led her through all that he was allowed to share. They had found a knife that was a visual match to the one in the evidence of Marlene's murder, but they had also found something else.

"Miss Scrooby, we found a plethora of items, all cataloged and labeled by Miller himself. The names on these items—tokens, if you will—all belong to women who are missing, or whose murders have gone unsolved. A few who haven't even been reported missing yet are found in this insidious catalog of his. Among these items was a charm bracelet labeled with the name Marlene Jacobs."

Eve began to cry. She had done it. Her friend, and all the other women that Derek had victimized, would see justice. They would be able to rest in peace.

"I took this bracelet to her family, who positively identified it as hers."

"Yes," wiping the tears from her face with a napkin, Eve nodded fiercely. "She always wore a charm bracelet. There wasn't a day when she didn't have it on." The kettle behind her began to whistle, so she stood to tend it. She took the chance to inhale a few steadying breaths while she poured the water into a ceramic pot that had belonged to her mother and put the lid over the vessel, allowing the tea to steep.

"That is exactly what her family said, Miss Scrooby. They also said something else."

She turned back to the table, listening to the detective tell her about Marlie's family.

"They said that the bracelet was a gift from you."

Tears sprang to her eyes again as she nodded with a wobbly smile.

"Yes, every birthday or Christmas, I gave Marlie a

charm. Once I found a little charm that looked like a book. Another time, it was a tiny car key when we turned sixteen and could drive. One year, her family took us all to the seaside, so that Christmas I secured a tiny shell to a jump ring that she could put on her bracelet. Our old teacher often took me to shop for them after my parents died. That bracelet will mean a great deal to her family. Thank you for taking it to them."

"That's the thing, Miss Scrooby. They told me that they wanted you to have it, and they sent their best Christmas wishes." He reached into the pocket inside his leather bomber jacket and pulled out the charm bracelet she had spent their childhood and teen years curating, commemorating so many moments of their friendship with love. Eve reached out in sheer disbelief, her shaking hand barely able to grasp the charm-laden silver chain.

"They wanted *me* to have this?" She could barely see the detective sitting in front of her through her tears.

"They did, miss. And that's not all."

Eve didn't know how on earth there could be more to this story, but she listened quietly.

"While we searched his flat at the permission of his landlady, Miller returned and was promptly arrested. He is being held in lockup while my officers continue our search."

Eve felt suspended in time, barely able to think or even breathe. Derek Miller had already been arrested. Was it truly possible that his crimes would never be repeated?

"Now," Detective Hallow patted the tabletop with his hands and stood. "You've got Christmas gifts to finish wrapping in there, and I've got mountains of paperwork to finish before I can head home to the missus for our Christmas, or it's my goose that's cooked."

Eve nodded in response, but couldn't find any words to express herself. She stood and followed him to the front door, opening it for her departing guest. Only when the noise from the street outside permeated the room, was she finally able to speak again.

"I—I don't know what to say, Detective Hallow. I owe you so much thanks. Words can never convey how grateful I am." Tears were running down her face again.

"You don't have to say anything, my dear. You were the one who gave us what we needed to bring justice. It is us who should be thanking you. Happy Christmas, Eve." He donned his hat and stepped out the door, whistling as he walked down the street. It vaguely occurred to her that he was whistling *God Rest Ye Merry Gentlemen* just like the delivery boy had been whistling the night before. This gave her an idea, which sent her running back to pick up her phone. Grabbing it from where it sat beside her teapot, she realized that she and the detective had never even had the chance to pour the steeped tea, but that no longer mattered. She opened the app she used for food delivery and started quite a large order from some local shops, keying in a large tip since she was submitting an order on Christmas Day. Scrolling through the delivery options, she punched in the return address on the envelope that Mrs Fezziwig had mailed. Just before she completed her order, she made one final selection: *choose my delivery person.* With a smile, Eve tapped the screen and sent her order through.

Just a few hours later, Eve stood at the front door to the Fezziwig home, nervously readjusting her grip on the cardboard box into which she had loaded some of the gifts purchased at the shops just hours before. They had not all fit, and some were still in the boot of her car in other boxes, which made her feel a bit silly about her shopping spree, but not enough to make her sorry that she had bought so much. A festive wreath she recognized from her recent trip here with the second Spirit adorned the entranceway, and she nervously reached out to press the button for the doorbell. A giggle escaped her lips as she realized that the family had programmed it to play *We Wish You A Merry Christmas*. She rolled her lips tightly for a moment, surprised by the sound of laughter coming from herself. It was not a feeling she had experienced in far too long and felt foreign to her. She hoped that soon it would be a normal occurrence for her again. The door burst open with a *whoosh* of air that carried the delectable fragrance of turkey and all the familiar sides that came with it. Standing before her was her beloved teacher, the woman who had held her when she cried for her parents, when she cried for her friend, and all the moments, both happy and sad in between. The woman whose motherly love she had also rejected when her pain became too much to bear.

"Oh, Eve!"

Before she realized it, Eve was being smothered in a fierce hug. She wrapped her free arm around Mrs Fezziwig and allowed herself to cry, hearing the same reaction from her teacher. With no questions asked, she was pulled into the house and welcomed heartily. Each child was introduced and offered the strange woman in their house a hug without even being asked by their mother; an embrace from a child being something else that Eve had not felt in many years. Perhaps not since she had been a little girl herself.

"I brought presents," she gestured awkwardly to the box she'd carried in. "I actually have more in the boot of the car, I just couldn't carry them in all at once."

"Presents? Oh, how lovely—but you didn't need to do all that! Nathan can bring them in for you, can't you, darling?"

"Of course I can, Ellie." The tall, thin man kicked off his slippers; a pair of garish reindeer with flashing red noses that made Eve laugh when she saw them. He stuffed his feet into a pair of galoshes by the front door before stepping out into the cold.

"Come set your things down, Eve. Tell me how you've been."

The two women sat on the floor in front of the Christmas tree, a little train chugging along a track at the base of it, whistling a merry *choo-choo* every few moments. Eve set the box down next to them and began handing wrapped gifts to her friend to place among the others. Mrs Fezziwig was sweetly aghast at the volume of gifts handed to her by Eve and protested kindly.

"Oh, honey, you didn't have to buy us anything, let alone so much!"

"No, I wanted to!" She shook her head firmly. "You asked how I've been, and I think you can guess. I've kept to myself and my gloom for so long, but now I don't want—no, I can't live like that anymore. I can't shut joy out of my life because I lost people that meant so much to me."

She reached for the other woman's hand.

"I still have so many people who love me and fill my life with joy."

The two women regarded one another for a moment, their eyes locked in unspoken communication. The older stroked the face of the younger with her hand like a mother would caress her child.

"I have prayed that you would let me into your life again. That your sadness would let you back into the world and make way for happiness."

A boot banging against the door prompted a child to open it, ushering in their father, arms laden with more gifts.

"Ellie! Look who I found parking outside!"

The two women turned to look at the two figures carrying more of Eve's parcels.

Charlie.

Their eyes connected instantly, shock clearly registered on both of their faces. Where she had expected to find anger, instead Eve watched one side of his mouth creep up into the lopsided grin that she had loved so much. That same grin still made her belly flop all these years later.

"Eve," he stepped toward her, the rest of his mouth joining the corner that had begun the grin. "You came." He walked closer to her, kneeling down and placing the box with the rest of the gifts next to the first one. She had known that he would be here. She had seen him when she visited with the Spirit, but seeing Charlie in person took her breath away. Here was someone who saw her in return, not someone who looked past her in her spectral state. She watched his eyes drink in the sight of her…his breath quickening at her nearness. She felt her body tense as she was close to him for the first time in seven years, her skin aching to feel his touch. Eve nodded mutely in response, neither one needing words to express their feelings at the moment.

All too soon, the moment was broken, shattered by the joyous laughter of the youngest Fezziwig, who caught sight of a tag with his name written on it. Of course, he would recognize his name written out with a former teacher for a mother.

"Timo-fee!' A chubby finger pointed to the tag in unbridled delight. His eyes squinted nearly closed with a smile that was nearly too big for his little face.

"Oh, this?" Eve lifted the oddly shaped package that had been so difficult to wrap. She had not thought to buy gift bags and had simply purchased several rolls of gift paper to wrap everything, which had proved quite the challenge with items such as little Timothy's stuffed dinosaur. She squeezed the gift a little bit, making the paper crinkle noisily in response, holding it out to the tiny child as an offering. He timidly took it and squeezed it like she had done, only he crushed the paper, squashing the gift against his chest. His little mouth dropped open in surprise, his previously squinted eyes now the size of saucers when the package elicited a mechanical *roar* from within the paper. He ran to the kitchen where his parents were tending the feast that was nearly ready to be served.

"Mama, mama, di-soar!"

"How did you know he likes dinosaurs?" Charlie asked her quietly, an inquisitive look on his face.

Eve shrugged shyly, blushing at his gaze. "I looked at Mrs Fezz—Ellie's pictures on social media and noticed that he always seems to have on a dinosaur shirt, so I made an educated guess."

"You always notice that kind of thing about people, Eve. You are a wonder."

"I haven't been kind to much of anyone in the last few years, Charlie. Least of all you."

Charlie brushed his knuckles against her cheek, his kind expression setting her more at ease. He reached for her hand and turned it over, kissing her palm like he always used to do. Her throat thickened, and she closed her eyes. She still loved this man so deeply. She knew from her experience with the third Spirit that he still loved her, but could he ever trust her enough to give his heart to her completely again? She would spend years rebuilding that trust, proving herself to him if only he would let her. She owed him that much after what she had put him through.

Yet one more ring of the doorbell brought the attention of everyone to the front entryway. Her phone buzzed in her pocket, and Eve pulled it out to glance at the screen.

Your delivery has arrived.

"Come help me a minute, Charlie?" She looked at him with a mischievous grin, all the fun they had experienced together in their past feeling much a part of the present, then jumped up, pulling him with her. "I've got the door, Nathan," she hurried past him to turn the knob. She greeted the delivery boy with a smile for the second time today. "Happy Christmas!"

The teenager blinked in shock. This strange woman had shown up twice on his busy Christmas day, and she could only imagine the story he would tell his family when he finally left work for the night.

"Happy Christmas. Again." He kept staring at her oddly as he handed over the box full of Christmas crackers, Turkish delight, tiny mince pies and Christmas puddings, a yule log, and bottles of mulled wine, Winter Pimms, and non-alcoholic eggnog for the children. "It was you? You already gave me such a large tip this morning. The one you left in your order was even more generous than before." He swallowed hard, obviously touched. "I don't know how to thank you."

"You thank me only by going home and having a Merry Christmas."

"Yes, ma'am, I will! Happy Christmas!" He poked his head in the door and gave the rest of the party a little wave. "God bless you!"

Little Timothy waved his chubby hand in farewell.

"God b'ess ev'ryone!"

The group laughed at his adorable proclamation, then filed to the dining room table where Nathan and Ellie had laid out the feast. Every bit of the table's surface was filled with rich and decadent foods. Steaming dishes of Brussels sprouts, Yorkshire pudding, gravy, dressing, roasted vegetables, and many other delightful items that made each person's eyes dance in hungry delight! The twins grabbed Eve by the hands and excitedly pulled her to a chair between the two of them. They told her all of their favorite dishes and pretended to gag when she asked if the Brussels sprouts were on that list, which made Eve laugh loudly, matching the glee around the rest of the table. Nathan Fezziwig stood and tapped a wine goblet with a spoon to gain the room's attention, declaring to all: "I've always wanted to do that." The guests groaned and chuckled in return, and one of the twins leaned her golden head to Eve's ear, whispering, "He says that every year." Eve chuckled in response. Mrs F—Ellie—had always loved silly jokes. It was no wonder that she had fallen for a man who shared her love for such merriment.

"I'd like to start by thanking everyone for coming tonight. I know we don't hold the largest or the swankiest parties in town, but Ellie and I are so happy that you've all come to grace our table. Your presence makes our Christmas Day that much merrier, filling it with joy, and giving hope to a wonderful new year in the immediate future. You have all been a part of our lives for many years." he looked around the room with twinkling eyes at all the faces before him. "Some of you are our blood relatives, and words can never express what you mean to us. Some of you have known us for longer than we have known one another. And some of you have been a part of our lives, even when we are apart." Eve felt her throat lock up. Nathan was surely referring to her, and while it could have made her feel awkward and singled out, instead it made her feel cherished and longed for, like the story of the prodigal son who was cherished while he was away from home. "We love each of you, and we thank God for you." He bowed his head and everyone around the table followed suit. He prayed eloquently, his Welsh lilt accenting his sincere words in a way that touched Eve's heart. In her hurt, she had not only shut out the world, but she had shut out her faith, too. She added one more thing to her mental checklist of the life changes she would be implementing from now on. The meal progressed with the chaotic passing of dishes, loud conversations that overlapped, and the *clickety-clack* of utensils on Christmas china as everyone partook of the meal laid before them. The group pulled apart Christmas crackers, read the corny jokes that were inside, and put on the paper hats. She felt Charlie watching her on more than one occasion, and a few times she dared to peek back. His eyes were kind, drinking in the sight of her, and he smiled when he caught her attention. Or at least, when he saw that he had her attention. Truthfully, her focus was on him for most of the meal. It was hard to ignore the man who still held her heart when he sat so close to her.

At the end of the meal, Eve began to help clear the table, but Ellie stopped her.

"No, you're a guest! Besides," she gently took a short stack of plates from the younger woman's hands and slid her eyes to the opposite side of the room. Eve followed her gaze, seeing Charlie playing with the children. "I think there's someone who would like a chance to be alone with you." Eve felt her heart pump wildly in her ears, her whole body growing fuzzy and warm. Charlie looked up from bouncing little Timothy on his feet and smiled at her.

"Children, come help with the dishes so we can open presents!" A flurry of small bodies rushed to help clear the table so they could soon tear into the brightly colored packages that surrounded the tree. Eve took a few shy steps in Charlie's direction, finding that he was already taking steps toward her, too. When they stopped, he stood close enough that she could smell his cologne. It smelled spicy and warm, the same scent that he always used to wear when they had been in love.

"Would you like to take a walk with me?" His hand stretched out invitingly, and her mouth suddenly seemed to be filled with cotton. All she could do was nod in the affirmative and put her hand into his. As their fingers brushed against each other, a jolt of electricity surged across her skin, igniting every nerve ending, making her heart race and her breath catch. Their rekindled connection brought a lingering warmth, a spark that promised more. It reawakened the passion and love that had once deeply tied them together. He led her into the front garden and out through the gate. Together they strolled silently along the picket fence, their feet making crunching noises in the snow as they walked side by side. Eve found their quietness companionable rather than awkward; as if they had not lost any time at all.

"How have you been?"

Charlie's voice was soothing, like honey's ministrations on the open wounds of her soul.

"I've...been. I suppose that's the best way to describe it."

Charlie nodded his head as if he understood.

"We lost a lot that night, you especially."

Drawing a deep breath, she jumped right to the heart of things before she could lose her nerve.

"I'm sorry, Charlie. For everything." She stopped in her tracks, almost forcing him to turn and look her in the face. Before she could lose her momentum, she opened the floodgate on everything she had held inside for so long. "Back then I didn't know how to manage my pain, and when you tried to help me, I drove you away. I hurt you in a way that no one should ever hurt a person—particularly the one that they love. I can never make that up to you. I understand if you never want to see me again after tonight, or if you want us to remain social acquaintances in the future. Words will never be able to convey how sorry I am, and how deeply I regret pushing you out of my life. We can never get those years back, but I'd like to at least be friends. That is, if you'll have me. If you'll let me."

For a few long moments, Charlie's eyes searched hers. She was unsure what was going on behind his eyes, and both feared and anticipated what he might say next. After what felt like an eternity, he reached for her hand again, gently rubbing the pad of his thumb against her knuckles, his touch tender and loving.

"I've never loved anyone but you, Eve. There could never, would never, be anyone else for me, and I would have waited a lifetime for this moment."

He took a step in her direction, closing the gap between them. Her breath quickened at his closeness, her skin alive with electricity once more.

"I would still like to marry you, Eve. If you'll have me."

"It was always you, Charlie. I wouldn't have anyone else. It could never be anyone else for me."

He slid his hand behind her head, weaving his fingers into her hair and drawing her into a kiss. Their time apart suddenly drifted into a hazy dream, as if it had never happened at all. The electric spark she felt when they touched became an explosion of fireworks at the meeting of their lips. The cold air around them that mimicked the pain that had held her heart in its icy grip now melted away, dispelled by a warmth that filled her heart with unexpected peace. The reunited lovers breathlessly ended their kiss, resting their foreheads against one another as they relished in the romance of the moment. The snow continued to fall around them, coating their hair and clothes in delicate, lacy petals of white. The two stood hand in hand, framed by the glittering starry sky amid the falling snow like a scene in a romantic film. Taking a deep breath and feeling truly relaxed for the first time in years, Eve was now filled with hope for the future, freed from all the pain and hopelessness that had haunted her past for so long.

It was a wild rumpus of a party, the Christmas spirit filling every nook and cranny of the house with joy. The children were giddy over each of their gifts, hugging Eve over and over again in thanks. She presented Charlie with the gift she had found for him, one she wasn't even sure that she'd have the courage to give. It was a knot of English oak that had grown in the shape of a heart. She had asked the wood carver to etch their initials into the knot, which he had done expertly before threading a scarlet ribbon through a hole in the top. Giving it to Charlie and seeing the emotional response displayed on his face, she knew that this trinket would someday be hung on their family Christmas tree every year for the rest of their lives. Eve felt herself growing truly relaxed in the presence of her friends: the people who loved her as if they were her family, and the man who would someday share a home with her.

Early the next morning, Eve woke before the sun

lit the sky. Babs had told her that she would report "bright and early", and Babs was always true to her word. If Eve wanted to surprise her, then she needed to get a move on. She loaded the gift basket into the passenger side of her car, buckling it into the seat belt with care. She wasn't taking any risks with the fragile items she'd wrapped so carefully. A satisfied smile hooked her mouth up toward her cheeks as she nestled in two envelopes that were sure to render her sweet assistant speechless. She hurried to sit behind the wheel and fasten her own buckle to drive the distance between her home and Babs'. She was almost giddy pulling up to their flat and walking to the front door of the building. Promptly at nine, Eve stood before the front door and waited, hoping that Babs would not call her until a few moments after 9 am.

Nine o'clock.

Nine oh-one.

A resident came out of the door, offering to hold the door for her. Realizing that surprising Babs at her front door would be even better than pressing the intercom button, she thanked the man and walked inside out of the cold. Checking the flat numbers to ensure that she knocked on the correct door, Eve slowly climbed several flights of stairs before reaching Babs' floor, then walked past several doors before stopping in front of Babs and Emmett's.

A brightly colored wreath was fixed with a large letter C for their last name—*Crachit.*

Nine-eighteen.

It was very unlike Babs to wait so long to call her, but that was perfect for Eve's little trick! She set the basket down on the floor just out of sight before deciding to stick one of the envelopes into the front pocket of her woolen coat. Preparing her most annoyed voice for her performance, Eve raised a fist and knocked firmly at the flat door. A voice inside called out, telling her to wait "just a minute", and shuffling noises approached the door.

"Who is it?" Babs inquired through the door, a cough accompanying her question.

"You're late, Babs." Eve kept the gruff tone in her voice, even when she heard her assistant gasp on the other side of the passage. The door opened quickly, and a tired and runny-nosed Babs before her, cloaked in a bed comforter.

"Eve! You—you're here! Why…how? I—I'm so sorry, I was already at my computer, but I didn't remember to call you yet," she stuttered and stared at her boss for a moment, disbelief painting her pale and sickly face like a thick layer of pastels on canvas. After what felt like endless seconds ticking away on the clock of life, Babs snapped back to attention. "Please come in, I'm sorry about the mess." She stepped back, opening the door more widely and gesturing for Eve to cross the threshold. There was very little "mess" to be seen. A few unwrapped gifts were proudly displayed beneath the tree—items the couple had given and received the day before. A rubbish bag was sitting nearby, overflowing with ripped gift paper that had been crumpled into haphazard ball shapes. On the table that sat in front of the sofa was Babs' laptop, already open and ready for work. A delicious smell assailed her nose, and she noted Emmett standing in the kitchen, watching her suspiciously. She could see that his hackles were already up, clearly bothered by the way his wife was afraid of her boss. He watched them warily, like a large dog watches an intruder.

"Please take a seat." Babs led her to a comfortable armchair with a little table beside it. On the table was a silver-framed photograph of the couple on their wedding day. Looking around the small flat, Eve could see photographic evidence of their lives on display everywhere. Birthdays, hiking trips in the forest, candid shots in their home…they all showed a couple deeply in love. A relationship that was worth caring for with tenacity. Lost for a moment in her own thoughts, Babs brought her back to reality when she began to speak again.

"I am so sorry, Eve. I suppose I made a little too merry yesterday, and it completely slipped my mind about the time and our morning check-in.

Christmas only comes once a year, you know…" She let the plea dangle for a moment, her voice shaking the words like nuts on a tree branch. "It will never happen again."

"No, it won't happen again," Eve glared at her harshly. "I won't stand for this sort of thing to be repeated, therefore," she reached into her coat pocket. From the corner of her eye, she saw guard-dog Emmett step closer to his wife, anger flashing across his face. "Therefore, I am about to raise your salary." She extended the crisp white envelope to her assistant. That woman sat across from her, eyes wide, face even more pale than before. Emmett stood behind the sofa, dropping the spatula he'd carried with him on the floor, smearing egg yolk onto the hardwood at his feet.

"You're doing what?" Babs finally croaked out a response.

"Babs, for far too long I have lived my life treating everyone in it like I am a tyrant. I wallowed in the sadness of my misfortune and made everyone who crossed paths with me to pay for my suffering. I won't be doing that anymore. You've worked for me for five years and you've never complained. You are an excellent assistant, and you are probably the only reason that I haven't chased away dozens of customers with my gruff treatment. I owe you a massive debt of thanks."

"I don't know what to say, Eve," she blinked several times, staring at her boss like a deer staring at an oncoming car in the road. "Thank you so much."

Eve shook her head.

"Don't thank me. I am just doing what should have been done in the first place. I haven't been paying you nearly enough in this economy. Perhaps when Queen Victoria was on the throne, but not now." She chuckled at her own joke. "I've also included a benefits package that I should have worked up long ago. Please, take a look and let me know if it's satisfactory."

Babs' eyes grew even larger, and she began to pull the papers from the envelope. Her husband mutely sat down beside her, his face a mirror image of the shock on his wife's.

"This is insurance? But NHS—"

"Doesn't cover everything," Eve interrupted. "Please let me know if what's covered is appropriate. I don't ever want an employee of mine to need something they don't have coverage for."

Babs read a few lines of the document before looking up at Eve with tears that threatened to spill over.

"This covers fertility treatments. How did you know?"

"Your love for Emmett is always so plain, and we've known each other long enough that I can deduce that you'd probably have a dozen babies together, so since there are none yet, I felt confident there was something amiss. I hope I didn't cross a line."

Babs shook her head, her tears flowing freely now. She leaned against her husband, who wrapped her in his arms, and looked at Eve.

"Thank you," his voice was tight with unshed tears, his previously tense expression now softened. "You have no idea what this means."

"I think it means everything to two people very much in love."

He nodded his head and kissed his wife's hair with gentle care.

"Give me just a moment," Eve stood up and dashed back to the door, opening it and grabbing the basket she had left in the hall. She took the few short steps back to the sitting area and presented the rest of her surprise to the couple. "You mentioned last week that Emmett had the rest of the year off work, so I thought a care basket would be in order."

In silent disbelief, Babs picked through the assortment of items that Eve had selected for them before coming to the second envelope. Upon opening it, her jaw dropped comically. Eve nearly sighed with relief that this was not the same jaw-dropping experience she had seen the night before.

"A reservation voucher?"

"Yes, I've booked an all-expenses stay for the two of you through the new year. I took the liberty of poking through your calendar, Babs. You check out the day before Emmett is due back at work after the first of the year."

"I don't know what to say, Eve." Babs stared at her for a long moment as if she was seeing someone entirely new. But, truthfully, she was. Babs had never laid eyes on this Eve before. The person she had worked for before Christmas Eve night was not the same woman who sat before her now, and Eve smiled happily at that realization.

"Don't say anything; it is my deepest pleasure."

Babs suddenly gave a little cry and jumped off of the sofa, dashing to the Christmas tree in the corner. Among the pile of neatly arranged unwrapped gifts, was a small paper bag with Father Christmas printed on it. He was bent down to hand a little girl a gift—a little girl that resembled Eve as a child.

"I got this for you, but it doesn't compare to the gifts you've brought here today."

Eve reached her hand into the bag, still touched that her assistant would think of her this way. She pulled out the little glass laptop she had seen Babs pick out back in Camden Town. Turning it around, she saw for the first time that it was emblazoned with the words *World's Best Boss* in hot pink glitter. Crying, she whispered her thanks.

"I don't think I deserve this. Thank you from the bottom of my heart. Oh! Please open that little brown box there." She gestured to the basket, and Emmett removed the item from the paper filling before handing it to his wife. She opened the top and pulled out the ornament that Eve had picked back at the same shop.

"This certainly calls for a picture!" Babs grabbed her phone and handed it to her husband before pulling Eve close. The two women gleefully held their ornaments close to their smiling faces, posing for a few moments until Emmett was satisfied with the shot.

"I hope you enjoy your time off, Babs. I want to see lots of pictures when you get back. In fact, if you ever want to work in an office, I'll have one set up for you. You can work wherever you please, be it here in your pajamas, or at a desk at my house."

Babs nodded her head and wrapped Eve in a bear hug.

"I would like that. No, I would love that."

After several hugs and heartfelt thanks from the two, Eve left the happy warmth of their flat and headed back to her car. As her phone connected to the Bluetooth, she decided to make a call. The voice on the other end was warm and made her stomach do flip-flops.

"Hello, my darling. I was just telling Dickens
that you were coming to see him today."

A happy *chirp* from her cat told her that he
would be as excited as ever to greet her when she
walked through the door. Shifting the car into
gear, Eve drove toward the future without a single
thought to the pain of the past.

EPILOGUE

ONE YEAR LATER

Eve tenderly laid a bouquet of roses in the snow, kissing her fingertips and touching the name inscribed on the stone.

"We did it, Marlie. Derek Miller was convicted on all counts last week, and all those women's bodies have been found and identified. Some are now buried not far from here, but I'm sure you already know that. Their families all sat in the courtroom where he could see them. Where he could see the faces of the ones who got left behind." She stood silently for a moment, wiping away tears that streaked her cheeks. "Thank you for changing my life, Marlie. Before and after yours. I can't ever repay you for the ways in which you have saved me. I promise to let my heart laugh, to live in the past, the present, and the future all as one. I promise to embrace the One whose Spirit inspires the joy of Christmas all year through." She stopped and chuckled for a moment. "And I promise to keep my appointments with my therapist. This one really keeps me on my toes." She took a deep breath, releasing it with a shaky sigh. "I'll never forget you, Marlene. And I'll spend my life remembering you with joy, not with sadness."

Blowing one more kiss to the gravestone, Eve turned away. She turned to the life that lay before her, the man who waited patiently with a smile on his face and an arm extended. Looping her arm through his, she laid her head against him, nuzzling the warm wool of his coat. She could finally look toward the past, present, and future with gladness and not bitterness. She could finally look at her fellow men with benevolence and not anger. Her heart felt full as she thought of the people in her life who loved and cherished her, making her life one that was filled with happiness. As tiny Timothy loved to say,

"God bless ev-ryone!"

About the Author

Jocelyn LaFavers has spent most of her life weaving captivating tales that blend romance and history with a touch of mystery. Her passion for storytelling shines through in every piece she writes, drawing readers into worlds filled with love, intrigue, and adventure.

Residing in the sunny paradise of Southwest Florida, Jocelyn shares her life with the man of her dreams and their four awesome kids. Together, they cherish the beauty of God's creation and make unforgettable memories on their frequent trips to Disney World. When she's not writing, Jocelyn can be found exploring nature, enjoying family time,

and finding inspiration in the everyday moments
that make life extraordinary.

You can connect with me on:
🌐 http://www.jocelynlafavers.com

9 798894 968940